THEATRE S

A PUBLICATION OF THE SOUTHEA

MW00513125

Theatre and Politics in the Twentieth Century

Volume 9

Published by the

Southeastern Theatre Conference and

The University of Alabama Press

THEATRE SYMPOSIUM is published annually by the Southeastern Theatre Conference, Inc. (SETC), and by The University of Alabama Press. SETC nonstudent members receive the journal as a part of their membership under rules determined by SETC. For information on membership write to SETC, P.O. Box 9868, Greensboro, NC 27429-0868. All other inquiries regarding subscriptions, circulation, purchase of individual copies, and requests to reprint materials should be addressed to The University of Alabama Press, Box 870380, Tuscaloosa, AL 35487-0380.

THEATRE SYMPOSIUM publishes works of scholarship resulting from a single-topic meeting held on a southeastern university campus each spring. A call for papers to be presented at that meeting is widely publicized each autumn for the following spring. Authors are therefore not encouraged to send unsolicited manuscripts directly to the editor. Information about the next symposium is available from the editor, John C. Countryman, Theatre Department, 5013 Berry College, Mt. Berry, GA 30149-5013.

THEATRE SYMPOSIUM
A PUBLICATION OF THE SOUTHEASTERN THEATRE CONFERENCE

Volume 9 *Contents* **2001**

Introduction

WHAT POLITICAL COMMENTARY, if any, is associated with "variety" theatre? What remains to be learned about the political objectives of Brecht's *Lehrstrücke?* What political power is resident in the satirical humor of Dario Fo's drama? How can drama teach political principles and entertain at the same time? What can we learn from Mordecai Gorelik's political/artistic philosophy that might inform contemporary practice? What was the impact of political theatre on Broadway between the wars? Is Thornton Wilder's *Our Town* the play we've always imagined it to be, or does it challenge the politics of its time? What is the role of theatre activism in raising consciousness about gender politics? These are only some of the questions addressed at the Theatre Symposium in April 2000, when scholars of diverse backgrounds from throughout the country gathered on the campus of the University of Tennessee-Knoxville for a conference titled "Theatre and Politics in the Twentieth Century." The papers delivered at the conference were a compelling mix of theoretical and practical, and the discussions they provoked were lively and informative.

This volume contains articles on a wide variety of subjects selected by members of the *Theatre Symposium* editorial board from among the thirty-plus papers delivered at the conference. Many papers worthy of publication have not been included in the volume because of space limitations. What remains is a fair representation of the topics covered at the conference.

The artwork on the cover was created especially for this issue by Berry College art professor, Dr. Tommy Mew. His mixed-media graphic is intended to represent the dynamic intersection of theatre and politics.

I wish to express my thanks to numerous colleagues who made this volume possible through their invaluable advice and assistance. These include former editors John Frick and Phil Hill and my associate editor, Noreen Barnes-McLain. Also, SETC Editorial Board chairperson Tom Stephens offered encouragement and support. Thanks are also due to Klaus van den Berg and his staff at the University of Tennessee-Knoxville Department of Theatre and to Margaret Harris and her staff at the University of Tennessee Conference Center for their organization and hospitality. Thanks also to Berry College and First Baptist Church of Rome, Georgia, for logistical support. Finally, Ruth Countryman's exceptional attention to the tasks of helping me organize the conference and facilitate the final manuscript is greatly appreciated.

JOHN C. COUNTRYMAN
EDITOR

Ladies Against Women

Theatre Activism and Satirical
Gender Play in the 1980s

Carol Burbank

I N *THE BONE WON'T BREAK* John McGrath proposes that political theatre contributes to

> a definition, a revaluation of the cultural identity of a people or a section of society. . . . Secondly, it . . . can, by allowing [threatened communities] to speak, help them to survive. Thirdly, it can mount an attack on the standardization of culture and consciousness which is a function of late industrial/early technological "consumerist" societies everywhere. Fourthly, it can be and often is linked to a wider political struggle for the right of a people or a section of a society to control its own destiny. . . . Fifthly, it can make a challenge to the values imposed on it from a dominant group—it can help to stop ruling class, or ruling race, or male, or multinational capitalist values being "universalised" as common sense, or self-evident truth. (142)

These guidelines offer an international perspective to illuminate the power of theatre as a political force.

Theatre and theatrical protest were central to the direct action movement in the United States. Yet, although activists created a remarkable range of performances and plays, theatrical activism has too often been undertheorized and undocumented, perceived as somehow less relevant to social change than speeches, sit-ins, and manifestos. When theatre is considered as serious activism, historians tend to focus on the most well-known, professional companies like the San Francisco Mime Troupe. Important as the plays and players of long-lived community-based companies are as exemplars of political theatre, theatrical activism was more deeply integrated into the direct action movements of the 1970s, 1980s, and 1990s than the study of scripted political theatre might suggest. Protest theatre offered nonprofessional performers a creative forum for presenting arguments in the streets and onstage, attracting media attention and galvanizing community identities in the conservative backlash that followed the cultural transformations of the 1960s in a practice I have called "intra-gender drag" (Burbank).

I am particularly interested in the ways countercultural parody and theatrical protest, in street interventions, rally entertainments, and cabaret performances, were used to counter the potent right-wing backlash that gathered national momentum during Ronald Reagan's presidency. Despite the early successes of antinuclear and environmental movements and other forms of social activism, the growing wave of right-wing activism based in Protestant moralism and global capitalism challenged or uprooted liberal and radical reforms and reasserted a nationalist ideology celebrating the nuclear family and its most conservative gender norms and economic policies. As a result, activists used the theatricality of momentary disruptions and entertainments to upstage the homogeneous naturalized spectacle of reasserted conservative normativity, expressing disrespect as a form of self-respect to create visible ongoing resistance. This self-conscious spectacle helped construct a strategic movement identity, which, along with other confrontational, lobbying, and educational aspects of social-change activities, represented a complex negotiation of escalating cultural conflict (Jasper). In particular, parody became a public performance of oppositional identity, a vital strategy to maintain what Nancy Fraser has called a "subaltern counterpublic" presence.

Cultural historian Joel Schechter argues persuasively that political satire is a powerful way of claiming agency by asserting comic irreverence against the political, rhetorical, and economic domination of the state. "The democratic impulse behind [a clown's] insistence on 'the right to make a joke' preserves at least a token of what the barbarians would destroy, even if it does not defeat them" (62). The collective experience of laughter results in a moment when "the individual feels that he is an indissoluble part of this collectivity . . . the people's mass body. The crowd in a theatre becomes a democratic assembly, with a clown rather than a king or president as its chief representative" (Schechter 17). The national protest theatre movement created by the feminist parody troupe Ladies Against Women (LAW) is a case in point, with the clown/satirists re-representing diverse leaders through the lens of gendered moralism in the face of an increasingly dominant conservative capitalism.

LAW began as an offshoot of an antinuclear agitprop group, the Plutonium Players, in 1977; their work spans 1977 to 1993, beginning with the year the Players started performing in Berkeley, California, and ending with their last performances on record. LAW was more than timely comedy and entertainment for progressives, although that in itself would have been an accomplishment because the collective combined so many issues in its feminist performance practice. The original troupe won awards for its stage work and performed all over the country in support of various progressive causes, simultaneously training and supporting a network of feminist protesters and performers who used their techniques to confront right-wing protests and presentations by groups such as Phyllis Schlafly's influential Stop-ERA movement and Jerry Falwell's Christian Coalition. LAW used stage and street activist reframing to present a fun house–mirror representation of conservative gender rhetoric, playing with oppressive gender stereotypes much as gay subcultures use drag and camp to articulate a space where alternative personal and collective identities can be explored (Burbank). This essay will describe the origins and street interventions of Ladies Against Women, introducing readers to the troupe's beginnings and the practices most imitated by feminist auxiliary troupes across the country between 1981 and 1986.

The Plutonium Players/Ladies Against Women developed in a very specific theatre community, built on progressive ideas about interrelated issues, cultural loyalty, identity, and activist citizenship based in the ideals and social experiments of the 1960s and the early protests of the direct action community of the 1970s. Although troupe members were initially more committed to environmental activism than feminist activism, the group was a diverse collective that started as conventional agitprop but developed its own style as time went on. It expanded from an amateur protest arm of People Against Nuclear Power into a much imitated professional improvisational parody troupe that was a staple of the political comedy circuit in the Bay Area and eventually in the national political scene. The supportive progressive communities of the Bay Area welcomed and nurtured LAW, and the creative mix of improvisational work and political activism shaped an aesthetic that seemed unique to San Francisco theatre workers, although activist theatrical satire ultimately became a part of national feminist vocabulary throughout the 1980s and 1990s. The power of LAW's serious-minded whimsy was its combination of agitprop, subversive gender performance, and entertainment. Through tours and auxiliary troupes the group extended a Bay Area aesthetic into the national sphere, feeding a need within feminist communities for an easily replicated, satisfyingly disruptive, and playful form of protest theatre that is still practiced by activists.

The improvisational performance of Ladies Against Women expressed the experiential friction between the real and ideal. The overt performance of the relationships among corporate capital, militarism, and gender roles articulated gender as the primary currency of capitalist identity, a radical idea even in feminist circles. The men and women of the Plutonium Players created ongoing, complicated parodic characters who became an intriguing hybrid of contemporary public figures, stock characters from popular entertainment, and prisms of the performers' own political and personal experiences and psyches. Men played hyper-masculine men, women hyperfeminine women, and all shaped their characters to criticize and explore the complacencies and shortcomings of progressive movements, as well as conservative activists and organizations. Their primary mise-en-scène was costume, reclaimed from the racks of thrift stores and supplemented by emblematic accessories, such as fur stoles with visible club marks and pillbox hats. Ladies Against Women reframed conservative ideology, as well as environmentalist and leftist political issues, within feminist ideology. This performative stance, coupled with their intragender adaptation of camp and drag techniques, created a cast of characters that modeled and dismantled patriarchal assumptions on many levels. Audiences who approved of their parody of conservative politicians, activists, and ideologies were also exposed to an entertaining feminist consciousness-raising strategy designed to offend opponents and challenge supporters. In its critique of public figures like Ronald Reagan, Phyllis Schlafly, Jerry Falwell, and their followers, LAW implicated the performance of gender stereotypes themselves as complicity with cultural and personal oppressions.

In a way Ladies Against Women used self-conscious feminist resistance as an exorcising process against totalizing ideologies submerged in conservative ideals of masculinity and femininity, arguably the religious right's most potent protection against social change. They used improvisational satire as a democratizing, media-grabbing strategy to maintain a resilient and easily reproduced public presence, invoking laughter to encourage a sense of toughness and persistence in the overlapping yet polarized and struggling movements of the left in the USA.

History and Performance Practices

The Plutonium Players developed from amateur comic relief and educational humor, beginning their cultural work at rallies and protests against nuclear power and nuclear armament in the Bay Area. Nuclear issues were, arguably, the central struggle for California's environmentally aware progressive community. In the 1970s and 1980s energy companies aggressively marketed nuclear power as the next viable source of energy, responding to fears of oil and coal scarcity and the need to develop a local and long-term source of energy that did not depend on foreign trade negotiations. Unless challenged, pronuclear advocates were unwilling to discuss issues of waste disposal or radiation poisoning. When pressured, they performed a confidence meant to reassure politicians, voters, and media representatives. One Pacific Gas and Electric spokesman, public relations representative Dick Davin, announced on San Jose's KXRX radio debate, "Plutonium—you could hold. You could put it on your breakfast cereal. Literally you could. And you could eat it" (*UC & Nuclear Arms* 1). In addition to pivotal proposed nuclear power sites like Diablo Canyon, where PG&E succeeded in building a plant despite concerns about fault lines and plant safety, the primary targets of the most vehement protests were Lawrence Livermore Labs and its affiliate Los Alamos Scientific Laboratory. These laboratories were managed by University of California researchers and administrators and were major sources of funding for energy research at the Berkeley campus (*UC & Nuclear Arms* 1). The labs designed and developed virtually all of the nation's nuclear weapons and were central in research on the neutron bomb (Freedman 8).

Bay Area antinuclear activists consciously used multiple strategies, including theatre, to raise awareness of the interrelated issues of military and environmental threats raised by nuclear proliferation, concerns about plant safety and efficiency, and waste disposal (Thompson; Hunter). Within the overlapping Bay Area movements the theatrical activism of groups like the Plutonium Players, and other troupes that became a regular part of public rallies, was part of a strategy of political embodiment as well as entertainment.

The Plutonium Players began working in 1977 as the "Information Through Theatre Working Collective" of People Against Nuclear Power of San Francisco. In the first year the troupe held no auditions, instead accepting all applicants, and insisted that all members cocreate what an official troupe history calls "informational pieces with intentional and unintentional comic elements" ("Plutonium Players" 1). Gail Williams describes the group's primary work as "microphone routines" and notes that everyone was expected to perform in, write for, and organize events (Williams 1). Although there were many models for rally performance, the Plutonium Players took their initial inspiration from the increasingly popular skit comedy cabaret. Satires of commercials or quick skits served as entertaining filler between speakers at rallies, in a format modeled on the then cutting-edge late night TV show *Saturday Night Live* (Williams 1).

Although the group performed in cabarets and Bay Area parks, producing several plays that were well received in the alternative press (see Donnelly), the most enduring performance practice became Ladies Against Women. LAW originated as a strategy the Plutonium Players improvised to advertise a "Stop the War Teach-in" on 8 April 1980 to protest the Soviet invasion of Afghanistan in December 1979. In exchange for a promise to publicize the event beforehand, the progressive radio station KPFA let the Plutonium Players perform in the teach-in, which included heavy-hitting Nobel Laureate speakers, as well as bands and folksingers. Gail Williams had done nontheatrical PR for antinuclear rallies and used her press list to advertise their protest "against" the teach-in, a "Rally to Stop the Peace" at Sproul Plaza, a historic site at UC Berkeley for protests. "I drew this weird drawing of people with top hats and jewels marching with their fists clenched, a parody of some sectarian socialist poster . . . printed on bright red, so you looked at it first" (Williams 5). The Reagan for Shah Committee was the central endorsing group, the result of a group brainstorm that combined California governor Ronald Reagan's bid for U.S. president with the U.S.-backed Shah of Iran's 1979 exile in New York. The *Daily Californian* reported that the planned rally was a response to the teach-in, noting that "speakers at this rally will include representatives from Mutants for Radioactive Environment, Berkeley Students for War, the Hexxon Research Fellowship, the Peace Resisters League, and Another Mother for World Domination" (Rodriguez 1). The imaginary antipeace activist groups built on existing groups like Students for Nuclear Disarmament, Berkeley Students for Peace, and the War Resisters League, clearly signaling the parodic nature of the event. They used their teach-in slot the next day by marching through the auditorium, masquerading as a group called Reagan for Shah Committee, chanting, "We want nukes, we want war, we think oil's worth fighting for!" ("Teach-in" 3).

The antipeace advertising rally was a more interesting event than their performance at KPFA's event, both in terms of entertaining parody and in terms of innovative political theatre. Establishing a tactic that would amuse and attract audiences and the press throughout the next decade, they kept their actor identities secret and represented themselves with great seriousness as representatives of their unlikely conservative groups. Williams reports that her LAW character was created during an early morning phone call from the national press, which called asking to talk with someone from the Reagan for Shah Campaign. "I said, 'Just a second,' put the phone down and . . . invented Virginia Cholesterol. I just answered questions and . . . improvised. . . . We had a few . . . weird slogans like, 'We want to give up elections because they pre-empt too much valuable television time,' and 'Climb into the coupe [coup] with the power under the hood: the Reagan for Shah Campaign.'" (Williams 6).

After their initial appearance the Reagan for Shah Committee, and eventually characters representing various other subcommittees, began appearing regularly in the street theatre scene of the Bay Area and the parks. By 1981, after Reagan's successful campaign, *Mother Jones* had picked up on the story and featured coverage of their satirical movement. "Activity continues," reported Zina Klapper, "despite internal debate over the question of whether Reagan for Shah (R4S) should now be known as Reagan *Is* Shah" (Klapper 10). The membership list had grown by then to include Science in the Corporate Interest, Union of Concerned Capitalists, the National Grenade Owners Association, the Future Dictators of America Club, the National Association for the Advancement of Rich People, and the John Wayne Peace Institute. Klapper noted that R4S "probably made its biggest splash at its own on-site [1980] Democratic and Republican convention rallies. Members distributed fliers that, right down to the tiny 'Slave Labor' [logo] at the bottom, urged attendees to 'Unleash the Fury of the Ruling Class.' . . . The 'toxic comedy and satire' street theater company, which ranges in size from four to nine members, then performed its 'song and dance show-and-tellathon'—the presentation of the R4S platform" (10).

Klapper reported the parodic campaigns of car-designer Lee (Iacocca) Iacaca, promoting "a tank that will get an EPA-estimated four gallons per mile, city," and of antigay activist Anita (Bryant) Tyrant ("Mothers, would you want your son in a trench with another man?"), and introduced Students for an Apathetic Society ("You may feel guilty about apathy, but how can the US possibly invade El Salvador if we aren't apathetic?") (Klapper 10).

Increasingly the male and female characters of Reagan for Shah and LAW staged public "counterprotests" at progressive rallies and counterculture parades like Gay Pride or the parody of the Rose Bowl, the Doo-Dah Parade. These protests were often framed as ridiculous exaggerations of gendered activities, such as an "Iron-In" or "Clean-In," or characterized by silly versions of conservative slogans, like "Sperms Are People Too." Characters from Reagan for Shah or appropriate subcommittees, which inevitably included Ladies Against Women, were visible performers outside the 1984 and 1988 Democratic and Republican National Conventions and became increasingly known in the national press and activist community networks. Characters included Ned Shrapnel of the Citizens for the Right to Bear Grenades. Sometimes appearing with his brothers Fred and Ted, who later became part of the cabaret act, Ned was a dull-witted rube who promoted "hand grenades for hunting, fishing and personal use only" (Klapper 10). Jaime Mars-Walker further developed A. Tad Slick, who was a press-agent type who served as emcee for many of the events. In addition to Mrs. Chester Cholesterol, the wife of a wealthy margarine rancher and the epitome of passive aggressive gentility, the Ladies included Mrs. (Edith) T. Bill Banks, a representative from the National Association for the Advancement of Rich People and the character Selma Vincent became known for. Mrs. Banks advocated that "the rights of rich people as a disadvantaged minority be respected. Because there's been a big attempt to take away their baby harp seal furs . . . and this is the ethnic dress of the American rich people, and it's important to their identity as it is for any culture" (Moore 120). Their most well-documented protest was their intervention at the 1984 Republican National Convention in Dallas, where they staged a bake sale for the deficit.

The challenge of satirizing the super patriotism that accompanies any staged national spectacle is to show passers-by that the performance is a different contribution to the highly costumed, celebratory political carnival of the convention. The performance strategy they chose, though, soon made their position clear, frequently when passers-by stepped closer to offer their support. Staging a bake sale for the deficit, troupe members sat behind a table scattered with Twinkies and other prepackaged cakes. They marked the cakes for sale at billions of dollars each and increased the prices as the day went on, offering improbable and tricky deals that they hawked to passers-by. According to Selma Vincent, their exaggerated costumes and coy in-character performances got multiple reactions, which reflected the usual levels of response in audiences they intended to offend:

> It was very strange there. Usually having a fur with wide-open eyes and a credit card on your hat is a clue. The slogans looked a little weird to them, but they couldn't tell for sure. They thought we might be renegade Republicans—moderates. Of course, there are lots of Republicans who very much want to get rid of the deficit, and they'd say "very funny—we agree with you." [Then] they'd come closer and see the budgetary pie with "Reagan's Foreign Policy: White Sugar, White Flour, White Power" written on it in Day-Glo frosting. Then they'd start to realize they were being offended. ("Interview" 9)

LAW's continuing performances on tour across the country and in Canada demonstrated the power of satire to break through feelings of isolation, disaffection, and frustration. As its popularity and exposure grew, the group began traveling extensively with its improvisational cabaret act "An Evening of Consciousness Lowering," which included appearances by what became known as the "Men's Auxiliary," turning gender hierarchies on their heads while purporting to educate audiences in antifeminist, procapitalist conservatism. Often, their tours included street actions and training in Ladies Against Women's satirical street theatre techniques. As conservative influence built through the 1980s, the troupe's value as a galvanizing, encouraging force in activist communities grew. Many audiences responded by forming auxiliary troupes, including troupes in Ohio, Louisiana, Georgia, Texas, New York State, and Canada. The Berkeley originators started a newsletter to keep auxiliaries informed and to share ideas. *The National Embroiderer* was part of a network of prochoice, pro-ERA feminists who used their personae to publicly and privately resist the totalizing rhetoric of gender that conservatives like Phyllis Schlafly used to persuade so many people that feminism was an unnatural and dangerous movement (Felsenthal; Schlafly). LAW's political parody was sometimes simply an entertaining interlude in a bleak period of radical activism, but it also served to maintain and galvanize communities that were growing increasingly isolated and frustrated.

Troupe member Jeff Thompson, most memorable for performing General Bull Run Lee, the head of a military boy's school, remembered a tour to Fort Wayne, at one time a center for the Ku Klux Klan and the site of contentious and divided leftist communities:

> Everyone [at our performance]—all the progressive, or lavender, or prochoice people, . . . nearly a thousand people, apparently a lot of the people hadn't talked to each other for a long time because of all these divisions, and they all stood up and gave us a standing ovation. People were in tears, they were crying. And they were talking to each other and seeing they had this common bond instead of their kind of sectarian life. And they were also, "Gee, I didn't know there were so many people who shared my outlook in this town." They felt so alone. (4)

Conclusion: Not Preaching to the Converted

No community is monolithic, and the divisive, passionate, radical communities in the United States are no exception. In social-change movements organized around issues more than core beliefs, it is dangerous to think of activists as converts. On both the far right and the far left, many subcultures collaborate and compete, with various results. Thus, it is important to understand political theatre as the servant of many masters and many issues. LAW member Gail Williams tried to dispel the dismissive stereotype of a preconverted audience that self-selects for people's theatre and activist performance: "People might assume we're 'preaching to the converted' but you can't assume that because you're all committed to one issue that you're committed to the others. Particularly with homophobia, we find that some people will laugh, others won't. People are learning from each other as they listen to the responses of hisses and laughter. Men in the audience listening to the rowdy dykes laughing and shouting are learning something subtle they didn't know before" (Jeannechild 24).

If we can resist the temptation to limit our understanding of political theatre, particularly the strategically rough, populist practices of street theatre and political improvisation, then we can begin to understand the ways theatrical activism unites and challenges multiple and overlapping communities. Protest movements used direct action strategies to create interruptive spectacles and heighten the disrespectful theatricality of public demonstrations and performances of alternative identities. In Erving Goffman's terms Ladies Against Women "rekeyed" conventional social frames by layering public events and identities with alternative meanings that have gradually and radically shifted the rules of behavior for men and women. LAW's interventions helped justify and activate a sense of urgency and community that maintained the alternative frames of reference even as they interrupted more conventional public frames put forward in service of dominant cultural ideologies. Through conscious theatricality they asserted an alternative public transcript, explicitly revealing the "hidden transcripts" of the dominant culture, to turn James Scott's term on its head. By making a public scene, and focusing media's attention on theatricalized activist space, they created a unifying, mobile rhetorical performance frame that made their point on several levels. They combined the real and the deconstructed ideal to create an often pleasurable confusion in the street's found audiences, who had to participate actively in order to distinguish the parodied from the parodist. Through this productive confusion, resolved by the subversive seduction of role play, Ladies Against Women's satirical social change networks helped activists negotiate the contradictions of struggling, and often failing to prevail, through a cycle of right-wing backlash in the United States. Even as they confronted conservative activists with the contradictions of their own identities, interrupting the right's performance of unity, LAW activists asserted and sustained a playful, fearless countercultural presence.

Works Cited

Burbank, Carol. "Ladies Against Women: Right Wing Drag." Paper presented at the Association for Theatre in Higher Education conference, San Francisco, August 1995.

Donnelly, Chris. "Battling Nuclear Power with Satire." *Phoenix* 8 (April 1980): 15.

Fraser, Nancy. "Rethinking the Public Sphere." In *Habermas and the Public Sphere,* ed. Craig Calhoun. Cambridge: MIT Press, 1996.

Freedman, Tracy. "Lab Is Driven from Obscurity: Livermore Becomes the Subject of Debate." *Daily Californian,* 7 May 1980, p. 8.

Goffman, Erving. *Frame Analysis.* Cambridge: Harvard University Press, 1976.

Hunter, Tom. "To the Editors." *Political Issues* 3 (June 1978): 20.

"Interview." *Off Our Backs.* Manuscript from Gail Williams's personal archives. N.d.

Jasper, James. *The Art of Moral Protest.* Chicago: University of Chicago Press, 1997.

Jeannechild, Penny. "Ladies Against Women." *Philadelphia Gay News,* 23 May 1985, p. 24.

Klapper, Zina. "Frontlines." *Mother Jones* 6.4 (May 1981): 1, 10.

McGrath, John. *The Bone Won't Break: On Theatre and Hope in Hard Times.* London: Methuen, 1990.

Moore, Anne. *Berkeley, USA.* Berkeley: Alternative Press, 1981.

"Plutonium Players: History and Purpose." In Gail Williams's personal archive. 1987.

Rorabaugh, W. J. *Berkeley at War: The 1960s.* New York: Oxford University Press, 1989.

Schechter, Joel. *Durov's Pig: Clowns, Politics, and Theatre.* New York: TCG, 1985.

Schlafly, Phyllis. "What's Wrong with 'Equal Rights' for Women?" In *The Phyllis Schlafly Report.* Alton, Ill.: Eagle Forum, 1972.

Scott, James. *Domination and the Arts of Resistance: Hidden Transcripts.* New Haven: Yale University Press, 1990.

"Teach-in." *Daily Californian,* 9 April 1980, p. 3.

Thompson, Arnie. "1500 Chastize [*sic*] University for Labs Link." *Daily Californian,* 6 April 1979, pp. 1, 27.

Thompson, Jeff. Interview by author. 7 September 1995.

UC & Nuclear Arms. Berkeley, Calif.: UC Nuclear Weapons Lab Conversion Project, October 1977.

Williams, Gail. Interview by author. 6 September 1994.

At "Cross-Purposes"

John Howard Lawson's *The International*

Jonathan Chambers

AT THE BEGINNING of his career, in the early and mid-1920s, American playwright John Howard Lawson was a leader in the theatrical avant-garde. Sworn to the task of revitalizing the American stage, and referred to at one point as "the Messiah of the new technique," Lawson, along with Eugene O'Neill, Susan Glaspell, and Elmer Rice, introduced new and experimental forms of dramatic expression that advanced American playwriting, leading it away from its dependency on the Aristotelian, well-made play form (Zimel 693). Identifying himself as an "artist-rebel," Lawson was not, during this period, overly concerned with offering any serious solution to the problems of bourgeois society.[1] Instead, he was principally driven by the desire to eliminate the constraints of realism and employ, in its place, nonrealistic styles and allegorical expression through symbolism in plot, characterization, language, and setting.

By the end of his theatrical career in the late 1930s, Lawson had evolved into a political revolutionary, dedicated to writing realist, proletarian plays that overtly promoted a socialist agenda. Barrett Clark's comment that Lawson was "probably the most consistent exponent of

---

[1]"Artist-rebel" is a term Lawson uses in his autobiography, "A Way of Life," circa early 1960s. Various parts of the unfinished manuscript relevant to this essay are contained in Boxes 94, 96, and 100 of the *John Howard Lawson Papers*. Hereafter, I use the following method to document materials drawn from this archive: *Lawson Papers*, followed by "B." (indicating box) or "Pkg." (indicating package), followed by "F." (indicating folder), followed by "p." (indicating page [when applicable]).

the left-wing drama" (706) indicates his importance as an artist who during the 1930s saw the stage as a platform from which to challenge the bourgeois political and economic order. Lawson's work during this decade certainly corroborates Clark's view of the playwright's significance. To be sure, his plays *Success Story* (1932), *Gentlewoman* (1936), and *Marching Song* (1937), which all overtly critique capitalism; as well as his associations with pioneering theatre companies with leftist leanings, such as the Group Theatre, the Theatre Union, and the Federal Theatre Project; along with his writings on playwriting technique and Marxist aesthetics, culminating with his groundbreaking book *Theory and Technique of Playwriting* (1936), clearly demonstrate that Lawson was, during this period, a leader among many left-wing theatre artists such as George Sklar, John Wexley, and Albert Maltz, who were seeking to effect change by painting realistic pictures of American society that would be instrumental in instigating a working-class revolution. Thus, over the course of two decades Lawson redefined his responsibility as an artist by rejecting his "artist-rebel" heritage and assuming, instead, the role of revolutionary.

A pivotal moment in Lawson's journey from "artist-rebel" to revolutionary came in the late 1920s while he was a member of the highly influential, although short-lived, New Playwrights' Theatre. In his unfinished and unpublished autobiography Lawson describes this as a time of "cross-purposes," a moment when he first struggled to satisfy both his deeply rooted need to continue experimentation with dramatic form and his ardent desire to advance revolutionary opinion (*Lawson Papers,* B. 100, F. 2, p. 368). His play *The International,* written in the summer of 1927 and produced by the New Playwrights in January of 1928, dramatically illustrates this struggle. Unlike his plays from the early and mid-1920s, *Roger Bloomer* (1923), *Processional* (1925), *Nirvana* (1926), and *Loudspeaker* (1927), where Lawson's primary intent was to "break down the walls of the [bourgeois] theatre"[2] by introducing new and experimental forms of playwriting, *The International* is an attempt on his part to satisfy simultaneously his own aesthetic demands and Edmund Wilson's call for liberal artists to "break down the walls of the present" (Wilson 234–38). In short, then, the writing and produc-

---

[2]Lawson first used the phrase "break down the walls of the theatre" in reference to his hopes for the 1923 Equity Players production of his play *Roger Bloomer*. It was, according to Lawson in an interview conducted by Robert Hethman on 25 April 1964, a phrase he used repeatedly in the 1920s. A written transcript of this interview is contained in *Lawson Papers*, B. 39, F. 1.

tion of *The International* can be viewed as a paradigmatic moment when Lawson's internal struggle, a ten-year dilemma that pitted his aesthetic sensibility against his burgeoning political commitment, was first manifest.

In this essay I will discuss the writing and production of *The International* as a paradigmatic moment in Lawson's career. My examination will include a consideration of the artistic and political impulses that informed the composition of *The International,* a reading of the play as a document informed by those impulses, and a reading of some of the critical responses to the New Playwrights' production of the play. In doing so I will highlight just one of the many moments in Lawson's journey down the "thorny path of commitment" (*Lawson Papers,* B. 96, F. 2, p. 356).

When The New Playwrights' Theatre dissolved in the summer of 1929, it was viewed by many as just another of the little theatres that had failed to find an audience. In retrospect the influence of the New Playwrights was considerable because it provided the bridge from the aesthetically centered little theatre movement of the teens and twenties to the more politically charged, workers' theatre movement of the early and mid-thirties.

On a more personal level, the two years Lawson spent with the New Playwrights proved to be a defining time in his life as well. Although his focus on aesthetic rebellion did not wane, his commitment to revolutionary politics became more pronounced. Lawson later remarked that his time with the New Playwrights served as an "introduction to *praxis,* to the world of action, involving an understanding of working people" (*Lawson Papers,* B. 100, F. 2, p. 383; emphasis in original). Still, when Lawson wrote his essay "The New Showmanship," the first in a number of unofficial manifestos for the New Playwrights, he stated in explicit terms that the theatre's central commitment was not to political revolution but artistic rebellion by way of the avant-garde.

The essay, which first appeared in the program of the Neighborhood Playhouse production of Francis Faragoh's *Pinwheel* in February 1927, opened with the bold claim that "the theatre of the future . . . is, here and now, an actuality." Lawson went on to assert that "the sole aim of the younger playwrights is to return to [the] honorable principles . . . of telling a story" that is both "pictorial and dynamic" and to attack the "flesh marts and somber commercial temples" (i.e., Broadway). He charged that "[t]he walls of these playhouses seem to have grown damp and musty with the gradual rot of stale sentiments, old jokes and dead repetitions." He concluded by declaring that although the expressionist movement had awakened American theatre to the idea of a "story-play," expressionism was just one "certain stage in the growth of native drama" leading to an "American type of show." This new method "utilizes . . . jazz, . . . sentiment and buffoonery," "is rich in plot," and "is concerned with real events which happen in the lives and hearts of [real] people." Above all, however, it abandons "realism" for "theatricalism" ("New Showmanship" 1, 4).

Clearly, then, "The New Showmanship" is a statement of an artist whose main concern is aesthetics. This focus was to remain central during Lawson's entire tenure with the New Playwrights' Theatre. Even so, by the autumn of 1927 Lawson and the other New Playwrights' central objective of returning to the "honorable principles . . . [of] pictorial and dynamic" theatre was broadened to allow for political overtures. Lawson's second unofficial manifesto for the New Playwrights, "What Is a Workers' Theatre?," appeared in the *New York Sun* on 12 November 1927. With this essay he demonstrated how far he had journeyed in a matter of months from the aesthetic-centered concepts of "The New Showmanship." In "What Is a Workers' Theatre?" Lawson claims that the ultimate aim of the New Playwrights' Theatre is "the presentation of mass plays, people's plays, done for workers at prices that workers can afford." He continues:

> Why introduce the killing wind of controversy into the greenhouses where flowers of pure art ought to be delicately nurtured? Because you cannot separate art from social problems without getting a pasty anemic byproduct without integrity or vitality. A writer for the stage who doesn't face America industrially and physically is shirking his whole duty as an artist. He can't conceal his lack of contact by handing out a thin knowledge of psychoanalysis and a few notions about love. And if he does his duty as an artist he has got to appeal to the people who constitute his real audience; not the stuffed shirts who come to the theatre for a few hours of mild diversion between dinner and dancing, not the few thousand spirits hungry for soul-fodder who patronize any theatre that labels itself "Culture."

Still, because "[t]he purpose of the stage is not to argue or convince, but to report—to see passionately and fully," and because it was "not the business of theatre to be controlled by any class or theory," the New Playwrights would not use their stage as a "soap box" for propaganda. Instead, they would augment their earlier goal of aesthetic rebellion by bringing to the stage a "revolutionary tone" and a "passionate vision of the current scene" that would reflect who they were as radical individuals ("Workers' Theatre").

The slight adjustment in focus that is at the heart of "What Is a Workers' Theatre?" was a reflection of international movements and events in both the theatrical and the political arenas. Artistically, this political slant positioned the New Playwrights as part of an international movement led by Meyerhold and Mayakovsky in Russia and Piscator and Brecht in Germany, who called for the creation of independent theatres that were interested in abandoning illusion and the picture-frame stage in exchange for "theatricalism" that would reflect the interests, the excitement, and the variety of working people. Politically, the shift to the left reflected a radicalization that was taking place among many intellectuals and that had been brought about in large part by the arrests, trials, and executions of Sacco and Vanzetti in Boston.

As it did for many American intellectuals on the left, the case of Sacco and Vanzetti and their subsequent executions had a profound effect on Lawson. Beginning in 1920, the same conservative forces that had inspired Lawson's flight to Paris as an expatriate entangled Sacco and Vanzetti. For the next seven years, as the two Italian anarchists struggled for justice in America, the American playwright struggled to find personal clarity and a theatrical form capable of expressing his vision of American life. The events in Boston in August 1927 brought both struggles to a climax. Sacco and Vanzetti were martyred to justice, and Lawson, stunned by the events, was consumed by a new passion to achieve clarity (*Lawson Papers*, B. 94, F. 10, pp. 318–19B).

Thus, although Lawson's focus in 1927 and 1928 would still be on the aesthetic and not the political, the struggle to find a compromise between these two objectives became more pronounced. Although the evolution of his thought is clearly reflected in the differing concepts presented in "The New Showmanship" and "What Is a Workers' Theatre?," further evidence of Lawson's movement toward a political focus can be seen in an analysis of his play *The International*, rewritten and performed following the events in Boston.

The idea for *The International* initially derived directly from newspaper headlines in the spring and summer of 1927. In April the Soviet-educated Chiang Kai-Shek turned against the Soviet Union and the left wing of the Chinese Revolution, crushed the Shanghai general strike, and began to slaughter his opponents. The disorders threatened foreigners, resulting in the deaths of several Europeans and one American. The United States, along with Japan, England, and France, intervened in support of Chiang Kai-Shek by shelling Nanking and sending a regiment of Marines to help occupy the international settlement of Shanghai.

Lawson, moved by the events in Asia, worked at a lightning pace and by the end of July had completed the first two acts of *The International*. Although his worldview was already pessimistic, the executions of Sacco and Vanzetti in August only deepened the playwright's pessimism. When he returned to New York in September, he was poised to write the third and fourth acts, in which war and revolution engulf the world.

The International tells the story of a future world war. It begins with two American businessmen, Spunk and Fitch, talking of the possibility of war in front of a gigantic map of the world on which "special attention is given to the great oil centers" (*The International* 9):

> FITCH. Sometimes I wonder if money is any good. . . . To me money means responsibility.
> SPUNK. To me it means power to do as I please.
> FITCH. In all parts of the world vast interests are at stake.
> SPUNK. My ethics about that are simple: make sure of our share and leave the rest of the problems to Washington.
> FITCH. I am not impugning the wisdom of our government. Men of high integrity are sailing the ship of state, but it comes down to a question of finance. If England forces our hand in the East, if lawless elements make trouble in Mexico and South America, we might be embroiled.
> SPUNK. I believe in peace as much as you do, but we can't stand still . . . spread . . . that's the big game.
> FITCH. Exactly, its international: in my youth, a railroad, a steamship line, a mine, they were independent entities; now the world is involved.
> SPUNK. That's why we must spread, take the map for a garden, cultivate it—
> FITCH. And war—
> SPUNK. Then if war comes, our country will be impregnable at least.
> FITCH. That's what they say in London, they say it in Berlin and Moscow. To be impregnable is a pretty dream, but I wonder where it leads?
> SPUNK. Dollars, and more dollars. (17–20)

Enter Fitch's son, David, a recent college graduate full of radical notions and dreams. David rejects his father's offer to work with the company, claiming that his map of the world "is painted in blood" (28). Instead, he longs for one of two things: "to see the working-class, be it . . . or see the world" (30). When Fitch and Spunk's business partner Henley enters with news of an expedition to see the mysterious Grand Lama of Thibet concerning newly discovered oil fields, Fitch sees an opportunity for David to "see the world."

The play suddenly changes from the realist representation of Wall Street to a highly symbolic style, incorporating statement and choral response, which imitate Greek dramatic structure. A chorus of eight stenographers, notebooks in hand, enters dancing and offers a "prayer" to "the machine" (46). The scene ends, and the play suddenly returns to a realist structure. David, now in Thibet, meets Karneski, a general in the Soviet army, who has been sent to Thibet to initiate a revolution for the Thibetan peasants, who will in turn overthrow the feudal regime of the Grand Lama. Armed only with an antiquated cannon, Karneski is about to fire when David enters. Despite David's pleas to wait, the cannon accidentally goes off, and the revolution begins.

As the explosion reverberates, the scene suddenly shifts to an office in Moscow. Rubeloff, a cynical and heartless Soviet official, and Alise, a refugee from Fascist Italy who has dedicated her life to the freedom of the masses, discuss her next assignment and the Soviet-induced revolution in Thibet. Alise longs to go to America, "the country of the Ford and the skyscraper," to aid in the revolution there; but Rubeloff refuses and, instead, sends her to Thibet to deliver a message to Karneski.

In Thibet Alise meets Karneski and David. Henley's attempts to buy off the Grand Lama have failed in the wake of the revolution. The first act ends with Alise, Karneski, David, Henley, and Tim, the "strapping American youth" who piloted David and Henley's plane, accused of aiding in the revolution against the Grand Lama, being bound by a dancing chorus of robed women and soldiers. The rest of the play comprises brief realistic scenes alternating with or augmented by choral odes that paint a picture of the revolution as it moves from Thibet to China to the Soviet Union and finally to the Western World.

Henley, who is tortured to the point of insanity, kills the Grand Lama. The rest of the captives escape in Tim's plane to China, where they crash in the desert, are saved by the British Indian army (who are later massacred by the "hordes of Asia"), and witness the introduction of United States troops into the conflict. While Karneski, following the orders of Rubeloff, chooses to lead the Russian army as it helps to "defend China against the greedy world of militarism," David commits to the revolution and with Alise returns to New York to aid the revolution (192).

In New York David and Alise visit Fitch's office, where they instill in the stenographers the revolutionary spirit. The chorus of women, in turn, sing the blues, in which they equate sexual freedom with the revolutionary cause, and dance off to Madam Miau's brothel, leaving Fitch "utterly alone" (220). In the brothel the prostitutes, led by Gussie, who is often visited by Spunk, join in the revolution. In the scene that follows Gussie, the servant prostitute, intuitively responds to the revolutionary call by strangling her master, Spunk.

At the beginning of the final act the war has consumed New York and left it in shambles, and workers have left their jobs. Still, it is clear that the revolution will fail because of the money and resources on the side of capitalism. Alise accuses David of being in love with her and not the revolutionary cause. In a flashback montage she remembers the events that led to her commitment to revolution. Suddenly, she is a young girl working in the fields of Italy:

> ALISE. The vines are rich on the hills, twining embracing the hills.
> CHORUS. Peace on our hills, peace . . .
> ALISE. What do you raise from the rich loam-land?
> CHORUS. Dynasties out of earth, sons of the home-land!
> ALISE. Grapes beneath our feet, rich from the vine, earth-smelling wine . . .
> CHORUS. Blood of the vine, to strengthen our sons!

Into this serenity comes Aretini, representing fascism. He symbolically takes the land from the people for the good of the state. Alise's calls for revolution are ignored, and the people commit to work for the state:

> ALISE. [Screaming.] I alone then, stand against you!
> ARETINI. You want the earth!
> ALISE. The whole earth, new and young again!
> ARETINI. Bah! Don't be absurd, you're a child.
> ALISE. I was, you made me something else.
> ARETINI. And you turn against me.
> ALISE. [To Chorus wildly.] Help me: do you want your sons to be killed? Destroy him now!
> CHORUS. Our feet are clay, rooted in the earth. . . . Dynasties out of the earth . . .
> ARETINI. They shall make sons of steel, suckled on blood.
> ALISE. I'll carry the flag then. [From her breast she pulls out a red flag, ties it to the gun she carries.] I too have a song!
> ARETINI. You are alone.
> ALISE. I sing a song, I carry a flag!
> [Alise sings the "International" in Italian. . . .] (244–45)

With that, a fascist soldier, at Aretini's command, stabs Alise through the palms with a bayonet, and her dedication to the revolutionary cause is secure.

As the flashback ends, fascist and communist forces converge onstage. Led by Aretini and Rubeloff respectively, two choruses stand on either side of the stage, exchange threats, and ignore the pleas for the people from Alise. In the end Alise's cries for help are ignored, and the people's revolution fails. As the play closes, David, mortally wounded, plants a red flag. Comforted by Alise, he huddles next to an overturned taxi and dies. In the midst of this apocalypse Tim steps out of the cab and asks drunkenly, "How do I get home? Christ, for love a' pity, where do I go home?" (276). With that a shot rings out, he falls dead, and the final curtain falls.

The International is an unrelenting assault on the societal forces that, in the opinion of many left-wing artists, were spinning dangerously out of control. Lawson's pessimistic view of the future, as well as the dramaturgy employed to convey it, was similar to those used in Gaston Baty's production of Pierre Mac Orlan's 1921 novel *La Cavaliere Elsa,* produced at the Studio des Champs-Elysées in Paris in 1927, and Piscator's *The Good Soldier Schweik,* produced at Piscator's Proletarian Theatre (i.e., Volksbühnen) in 1928. However, unlike his international peers Lawson shows little partiality in this assault, attacking forces on the political left, middle, and right. The aggressive American capitalists Spunk and Fitch, who speak of "spread[ing]" and "cultivat[ing]" the world, are neatly juxtaposed against the icy communist Rubeloff, who dreams of fomenting world revolution, and the sadistic fascist Aretini, who thrives on military conquest. The people of the world are mere pawns caught in the middle of a deadly game played by these various government regimes that are willing to destroy anyone to insure victory. This dreary outlook accords with the pessimistic view of the world's future that Lawson held at that time: the end of civilization is at hand, and there is no hope (*Lawson Papers,* B. 100, F. 2, p. 367). This sense of doom is most obvious in his two main characters, David and Alise.

Although the character Tim clearly symbolizes the working class doomed to die at the hands of bourgeois-inspired destruction, it is the middle-class David who offers the best indication of the playwright's thought at this time. Lawson wrote, "I felt intuitively that a second world catastrophe was certain. The young middle-class intellectual who dies as bombs fall on New York is me. I saw no hope in revolution, only destruction and the death of millions" (*Lawson Papers,* B. 94, F. 10, p. 327A). The character Alise further reflects this pessimism. Although she seeks truth, she is helpless. There is only death and the hope that the cause will someday be rectified. As a result of this positioning, she becomes a lifeless figure. Her total dedication to the revolution has no human motivation, and her actions have no rational purpose. At the end, when David dies in her arms, she can only speak in rhetoric: "I carry change like a serpent in my breast." In the end she can find meaning for life only in the revolution:

> ALISE. We are pilgrims seeking a flag. . . .
> DAVID. Plant a flag here . . . New York . . . a bee-hive . . . a pyramid of stone. . . .
> ALISE. It will grow higher, we will be dead. . . . (274–75)

Alise's half-optimistic vision is the only expression of hope in the whole play. It is cut short, however, by Tim's being shot dead in the street.

As was becoming standard for Lawson's plays, the critical response to *The International* was anything but kind. The mainstream press was, for the most part, merciless. Steven Rathburn, writing for the *Brooklyn Eagle,* claimed that "the dramatic bombshell of a world revolution was a dud." In the *Evening World* E. W. Osborn pondered the playwright's pessimistic view of the future: "Apparently Mr. Lawson finds the world on the brink of something or other, and means to set labor force as a means of stopping whatever is going on." Similarly, in his review for the *New York Journal,* "Mr. Lawson Writes Another Ear-Splitting Upheaval," John Anderson described the play as a "crowded, inchoate, and exquisitely tiresome rookus" and charged Lawson with "confus[ing] the stage with the soapbox" and "intellectual vertigo." Alexander Woolcott was the most acidic and blunt, referring to it in a short review as "excruciatingly uninteresting."

A few mainstream critics saw promise and progress amid the many problems. Brooks Atkinson applauded Lawson's commitment to new forms. "In both *Roger Bloomer* and *Processional* [Lawson] essayed new forms, and in *The International* he bursts still another stage wall." Similarly, Gordon M. Leland, a longtime admirer of Lawson's work, referred to Lawson as "a writer of modern philosophy in expressionistic play form" (11).

Given the pessimistic view of the revolution and the unflattering portrayal of the Soviet Union, it is not surprising that the left-wing press found great fault in *The International.* Most notably, Sender Garlin of the *Daily Worker,* although commending Lawson for his "honest and courageous attempt to treat a subject which thus far has been strictly taboo in the American bourgeois theatre," denounced the playwright for his "intellectual confusion" and "romantic" notions of the revolution ("Lawson Play"). A few days later fellow New Playwright John Dos Passos wrote a letter to Garlin defending Lawson and the play:

> [*The International* is a] very personal and subjective emotional outburst expressing one man's feelings under the impact of our world today. [It] is a broad cartoon of the dynamics of current history. It uses all the stock cartoon figures and ideas, warping them to its own purpose. Because it is the first time this has been done on the American stage everybody comes out flustered and starts cursing the play out for not being "realistic" or a number of things that it never intended or wanted to be. (Letter to the Editor, 20 January)

The next day, in a lengthy response, Garlin countered that although "the technique in *The International* [was] interesting and significant," he still found the play to be "based on misconceptions of the nature of the world revolution and of the key figures that dominate its operations" ("Response"). A week later Dos Passos fired back. He objected to Garlin's comments not because they disputed the value of the play but because they seemed "to be written from the same angle as those in the capitalist press, the angle of contemporary Broadway 'realism'" (Letter to the Editor, 28 January).

While the Garlin–Dos Passos debate raged in the press, Lawson was visited by Joseph Freeman, editor of the *New Masses*. During a "long but friendly" visit Freeman pointed out the ideological errors in *The International*. At the time Lawson found it strange that Freeman, who was noted for his aesthetic sensibilities, made no reference to the artistic values in the play. Lawson recalled the discussion: "We talked at cross purposes. I spoke of the need to break the mold of 'bourgeois' forms and sterile emotions, and Joe answered with an analysis of the world situation. I listened carefully, but even in political terms, I could not accept his formulations. I believed my vision of doom was nearer to reality than his faith in the triumph of 'the masses'" (*Lawson Papers*, B. 100, F. 2, p. 368A). Ironically, over time Freeman came to reject the lessons he sought to teach Lawson, and Lawson came to accept them and teach them to others. For the time being, however, Lawson was unable to embrace the idea of a working-class revolution, and his commitment to artistic rebellion remained a central concern.

Even so, by the summer of 1928 the singular commitment to artistic rebellion that had governed Lawson's work was, on some level, being threatened. In May, as one of his final acts as a functioning member of the New Playwrights, Lawson wrote and edited the copy for a pledge pamphlet that was sent to all season-ticket holders. The message on the pamphlet demonstrates the playwright's developing internal conflict. At the top of the first page, under the heading "The New Playwrights' Theatre," are two phrases presented as credos: "experiment in playwriting and play production," and "pledged to be a stronghold of liberal and radical opinion." Beneath these two phrases Lawson wrote, "We must keep up this double work of innovation and ideas" (Leaflet for Pledges). It seems then, that when Lawson departed for Hollywood later that summer, he took with him a twofold ideal, to be both an artist-rebel and a political radical. Although he did not yet have a clear understanding of how to reconcile these two goals, he was consumed by "a thirst to find my place in the world—the part of the world in which I intended, whether I consciously knew it or not at the time, to live my life" (*Lawson Papers*, B. 100, F. 2, p. 387).

Works Cited

Anderson, John. "Mr. Lawson Writes Another Ear-Splitting Upheaval." Review of *The International*. *New York Journal*, 16 January 1928, p. B2.

Atkinson, Brooks. Review of *The International*. *New York Times*, 16 January 1928, p. 24.

Clark, Barrett H., and George Freedley, eds. *A History of Modern Drama*. New York: Appleton Century, 1947.

Dos Passos, John. Letter to the Editor. *Daily Worker*, 20 January 1928, p. 4.

———. Letter to the Editor. *Daily Worker*, 28 January 1928, p. 6.

Garlin, Sender. "Lawson Play an Ingenuous Drama of the Revolution." Review of *The International*. *Daily Worker*, 16 January 1928, p. 4.

———. "Response to John Dos Passos." *Daily Worker*, 21 January 1928, p. 6.

Lawson, John Howard. *The International*. New York: Macaulay, 1927.

———. "John Howard Lawson Papers." Collection 16, Morris Library. Southern Illinois University. N.d.

———. Leaflet for Pledges, New Playwrights' Theatre. April 1928. *Lawson Papers* Pkg. 1.

———. "The New Showmanship." *Pinwheel* Program, February 1927.

———. "What Is a Workers' Theatre?" *New York Sun*, 12 November 1927. *Lawson Papers* Pkg. 1.

Leland, Gordon M. Review of *The International*. *Billboard*, 28 January 1928, pp. 11, 89.

Osborn, E. W. Review of *The International*. *Evening World*, 16 January 1928, p. 12.

Rathburn, Steven. Review of *The International*. *Brooklyn Eagle*, 16 January 1928. *Lawson Papers* Pkg. 1.

Wilson, Edmund. "An Appeal to Progressives." *New Republic*, 14 January 1931, pp. 234–38.

Woolcott, Alexander. Review of *The International*. *The World*, 16 January 1928. *Lawson Papers* Pkg. 1.

Zimel, Heyman. "Messiah of the New Technique." Review of *Processional*. *American Hebrew*, 25 March 1927, p. 693.

Surpassing Representation

The Changing Character of the Collective in *Lehrstücke* by Brecht and Müller

Steve Earnest

MANY COMPARISONS have been drawn between the two German dramatists Bertolt Brecht and Heiner Müller. Given the form and content of his works, Müller is clearly a part of the post-Brechtian tradition both as a playwright and as a director. However, as has been noted on several occasions, Müller's work embodies an aesthetic Brecht was not successful in achieving because of political and artistic parameters. This essay will explore certain political aspects that influenced the *Lehrstücke* of both Bertolt Brecht and Heiner Müller, specifically the dramatic shift of focus from the individual, Cartesian figures of the Brechtian *Lehrstücke* to the collective, dehumanized character of Müller's *Lehrstücke*.

Literally "teaching plays," *Lehrstücke* are short, didactic works meant to be performed by students (preferably nonactors) as a part of their orientation to Marxist ideals. No audience is expected or necessary within the concept of the *Lehrstücke;* the event is self-contained with the participants themselves taking on the roles of audience and performer. The overriding principle of the *Lehrstücke* is that moral and political lessons contained in the plays can best be learned through participation in actual production. Brecht's additional qualifying statements are as follows:

> [Whereas] the Aristotelian play is to show the world as it is, the learning play's task is to show the world as it changes, and also how it may be changed. It is common truism among the producers and writers of the former type of play that the audience, once it is in the theatre, is not a number of individuals but a collective individual, a mob, which must be and can be reached only through its emotions; that it has the mental im-

maturity and the high emotional suggestibility of a mob. The latter theatre (Brecht's theatre) holds that the audience is a collection of individuals, capable of thinking and reasoning, of making judgements in the theatre; it treats it as individuals of mental and emotional maturity, and believes it wishes to be so regarded. (*Brecht on Theatre* 79)

The best examples of works in this regard include *The Flight of the Lindberghs*, *The Exception and the Rule*, *The Measures Taken*, and the two school operas *He Who Says Yes* and *He Who Says No*, all written between 1929 and the early 1930s, a period of great political and social turmoil in Germany.

The *Lehrstücke* lie at the very heart of Brechtian theatre, yet Brecht had only begun to experiment in this vein when he was forced to flee Berlin in 1933. The criticism Brecht received from both German and Russian Communist Party members regarding the *Lehrstücke* is well documented; critics of Brecht's theatre aesthetic stated that the works were too formalistic, too vague, and too personal (Doe 294). According to critics from the party, none of the *Lehrstücke* promoted collective society, nor were they presented in a form that was easily understandable by the masses, two of the major criteria of social-realist works of art. On his return to Germany in 1948 Brecht had more firmly solidified his theories regarding epic methods of production, including his ideas concerning the *Lehrstücke*. Brecht had hoped that the newly formed German Democratic Republic (GDR) would be more receptive to his "progressive" ideas about socialist art. However, as Brecht returned to "business as usual," staging *Mother Courage* at the Deutsches Theatre in 1949, he was faced with severe criticism, this time from the East German social realists. Led by dramatist Frederick Wolf, critical attack targeted Brecht's play on the basis that the title character did not seem to change or to gain a new social insight by the play's end. Brecht's epic modes of production were labeled objectivist by the Central Committee of the Socialist Party, which eventually denied production of his play *Last Days of the Commune* in 1952. Several other challenges were brought against the content of Brecht's plays, as well as against his production techniques, all of which resulted in a series of "Stanislavski" conferences later in 1952, which debated ideas about form and content as related to theatrical production. Brecht wrote no additional *Lehrstücke* after he returned to Germany, although he continued to write and alter his theories regarding theatre up to the time of his death, including a statement about the *Lehrstücke*, describing the plays not as learning plays but as "limbering up exercises for those athletes of the spirit that good dialecticians must be" (Doe 295).

Although Brecht had continually argued for a more experimental social-realist technique, many of the changes that he proposed did not gain official acceptance until 1956, the year of his death. Therefore, the bulk of his ideas concerning epic theatre, alienation, and *Lehrstücke* remained shackled by strict guidelines imposed by the East German social realists (Frederick Wolf, Fritz Erpenbeck, and others) who were backed by the Socialist Unity Party of Germany (SED). As dictated by the State Commission for Artistic Affairs (a branch of the SED), theatrical events should be "photographic castings of everyday reality," with recognizable human characters undertaking events and actions based in the material world (Sontheimer 126). Clearly, works that encouraged actions of a highly formalized nature such as the shifting of character from one actor to the other did not fall under this category and were discouraged or disallowed completely.

Perhaps the best example of Brechtian *Lehrstücke* is *The Measures Taken*, which deals with a group of Russian agitators who, while working in China to promote communism, eventually kill their Chinese guide, who cannot accept the inhuman actions proposed by the agitators. Brecht's moral lesson (borrowed from Kleist) is espoused when the young Chinese guide is asked to accept his death as a necessary part of the growth of communism, which he does. The play's action incensed both German and Russian Communist Party members, who denounced the work as "a petty-bourgeois intellectualist piece of work" that was the exact opposite of Lenin's teachings. Members of the Communist Party felt that Brecht's play showed communism as cold and heartless and that it did nothing to affirm the communist way of life (Doe 289). *The Measures Taken* was never performed in the GDR.

As a committed Marxist, Brecht had hoped that the theatre of East Germany would find its own sophisticated means of expression, more effective than "propagandistic representations of contemporary social reality clothed in Stanislavski technique" (Rouse 58). However, because of the limitations of social-realist production standards Brecht was never able to achieve a true sense of collective performance. Therefore, despite a fair amount of discourse and published material dealing with character division and altered modes of playing, Brecht's plays, including the *Lehrstücke* were written and performed with recognizable characters and situations. True, all of the works were performed by an ensemble, with an onstage chorus occasionally providing commentary, but the focus of Brecht's *Lehrstücke* is clearly on decisions and actions taken by individuals (shown as past events that drive the action of the play). To again use *The Measures Taken* as an example: the four agitators, themselves individuals with assigned names (albeit "demonstrated" within the format of Brechtian performance by members of the company), report the past events to the Control Chorus, who react to the demonstration and discussion in human terms. During the second scene, "The Effacement," each of the characters is given a mask, thus briefly blurring their identities. As the masks are placed on the agitators' faces, the "Head of the Party House" addresses them: "And therefore from this moment on you are no longer no one; but rather from this moment on, and in all probability until your disappearance, you are unknown workers, fighters. Chinese born of Chinese mothers, yellow skinned, who in sleep and delirium speak only Chinese. (They reply 'yes.') In the interests of Communism you agree with the advance of the proletariat of all lands. You agree with World Revolution" (Brecht, *Measures Taken* 12). Although their humanness is "blurred" or masked temporarily, the fact remains that it exists—they begin the play as individual human beings, and as the play progresses their sense of humanity and individuality diminishes. Instances of human emotion are displayed throughout by the young Chinese guide, who attempts to rouse a group of workers that is being abused. The guide finally allows his personal values to overtake him when he refuses to accept communist ideals, and the resultant emotional display ultimately costs him his life. Individual decisions and human interaction drive the action of the play.

The focus on individual decisions by Brecht contrasts with later experimentation with the *Lehrstücke* form by East German playwright Heiner Müller, who, as a post–*Neue Sachlichkeit* writer, was able to escape much of the criticism regarding theatrical form that continually plagued Brecht. Before discussing Müller's use and critique of the Brechtian model, it will be useful to point out the changes in the East German system that allowed for a more objective approach to social-realist works of art.

Following the debate over form that had prompted the Stanislavski conferences of 1952, the East German dramatist Peter Hacks published a series of articles in *Neue Deutsche Literatur* that proposed a more dialectical view of realism based more evenly on the theories of Brecht and the Marxist philosopher Georg Lukacs. According to Hacks, a dramatist could chart one of two paths: by dramatizing the historical process in action or by using poetic material to anticipate the course of history. Hacks noted that the drama of East Germany was poised to become more formally sophisticated because the East German society had embarked on a new quest for self-advancement. The direction suggested by Hacks and other artists became part of a movement known as the *Neue Sachlichkeit,* or New Objectivity, which emphasized removal of objects from contextual relationships, favored collage-like assemblage of "particles of experience," and a new mental relationship with the world of objects. By 1957 the SED's official position toward drama allowed for new forms and experimentation. Thus two forms of drama became acceptable in the GDR: the more traditional socialist realism and an experimental theatre based on the theories of Brecht (Huettich 27).

Heiner Müller began his career as a poet and dramatist during the early years of the *Neue Sachlichkeit*. Although Müller escaped the criticism regarding formalist production means that had hounded Brecht, he was by no means a writer who stayed in favor with Socialist Party authorities. In fact, Müller's battles with GDR cultural authorities began early in his career as he was expelled from the Writers Union in 1961, when his production of *The Resettled Woman* was closed by GDR authorities after the dress rehearsal. Several of his productions were canceled and/or banned from the stage; *The Construction Site* (1965) was disallowed because of its negative portrayal of socialist society and *Quartet* (1980) was deemed pornographic by GDR authorities. *Mauser,* a critique of *The Measures Taken,* was never allowed production in the GDR, premiering instead in Austin, Texas, in 1971. The play comments not only on the fallacies implicit in the content of Brecht's play but also on the form of Brechtian *Lehrstücke* that Müller found replete with "Marxist textbook ideology" (Müller, *Battle* 8). *Mauser* deals with a "semihistorical" account of an ordinary Russian citizen/revolutionary who fails in his duty to carry out the mission of the revolution. The accused citizen, known only as A, becomes so involved in the process of executing "enemies of the revolution" that he launches into a fit of orgiastic killing. By allowing himself to deviate from his assignment, as he becomes engrossed in the process of killing, he places himself at immediate odds with the party. The result is a trial-like situation where citizen A is confronted by society, ideology, and the "official positions" taken by both leaders and individual citizens. For his actions citizen A is sentenced to die, and like both the Chinese guide in *The Measures Taken* and the young boy in *He Who Says Yes,* he is coerced not only into accepting his death but into accepting that his death is a necessary part of the revolutionary cause.

Mauser was scheduled to premier in the GDR in 1972 at the Magdeburg State Theatre as part of a week of Soviet and Soviet-influenced theatre. Two weeks into the rehearsal process Intendant Hans Diether Meves was informed by the East German ministry of culture that rehearsals for *Mauser* had been terminated. The written notification stated that "the publication and distribution of this text within the territory of the German Democratic Republic is forbidden" (Müller, *Krieg Ohne*

Schlacht 258). Critics felt that Müller's play presented a Stalinist version of Marxism by portraying the revolution as an "objective process occurring outside the will of human beings," thus presenting what they defined as "counter revolution" (Müller, *Krieg Ohne Schlacht* 259). Additionally, critics were disturbed by the level of revolutionary will and political activism, both of which countered traditional Marxist views stressing the dependence of political change on maturing of social and economic forces. Considering Stalin's Five-Year Plan, which included the collectivization of agriculture and other areas of society, the content of *Mauser* is startling. The Chorus begins the work, speaking a passage that it repeats either in its entirety or in fragments on five other occasions during the short dramatic work. The passage reads:

> You have fought at the front of the civil war. The enemy hasn't found any weakness in you. We haven't found any weakness in you. Now you yourself are a weakness the enemy must not find in us. . . . Do your work now at the last place the Revolution appointed you to, the place you won't leave on your feet. At the wall which will be your last one. As you have done your other work. Knowing, the daily bread of the Revolution in the city of Witebsk as in other cities is the death of its enemies. Knowing, even the grass we must tear it up so it will stay green. (Müller, *Battle* 122)

This initial speech is a microcosm for the entire play, with its poetic structure, internal repetition, and official, doctrinal reportage. The speech is directed to the character A, who stands on trial for "killing with his own hand, not enemies, and not by appointment." A's work for the revolution consisted of eliminating dissent and opposition, and not unlike the type of pathological killing that took place during the Five-Year Plan, he viewed his work as a necessary service to the revolution. A lacks human feeling and emotion, and is therefore converted into a killing machine, noting that the "act of killing" had taken over his entire persona. A states:

> My hand dispensed death like it wasn't my hand, and the killing was a killing of another kind, and it was work like no other work, and at night I saw my face that looked at me with eyes not my own, out of the mirror, many times cracked from the shelling of the city many times taken. And during the night I was not a man, burdened with those killed over seven mornings, my sex the revolver that dispenses death to the enemies of the Revolution, facing the quarry (Müller, *Battle* 126).

A's break with the party ideology of *Mauser* occurred when his internally based decision (his will) took precedence over the external, objective process of the revolution. A admits, "It isn't enough for me to kill what must die so the Revolution will triumph and the killing end but it shouldn't be here anymore and be nothing forever and disappear from the face of the earth, a clean slate for those who will come" (Müller, *Battle* 129). As punishment for his emotional, undisciplined act, A is now faced with the ultimate revolutionary task—to pay for his mistake with his life and to acknowledge the fact that his death is a necessary part of the revolution. In answering the charges A is trapped not only by the reflexive/repetitive answers of the Chorus but also by the repetitive structure of the text:

> A: I have done my work
> CHORUS: Do your last work.
> A: I have killed for the Revolution.
> CHORUS: Die for her.
> A: I have committed a mistake.
> CHORUS: You are a mistake.
> A: I am a human being.
> CHORUS: What is that?
> A: I don't want to die.
> CHORUS: We don't ask if you want to die. The wall at your back is the last wall, at your back. The Revolution doesn't need you anymore. It needs your death. But until you say yes to the no that has been pronounced on you, you haven't finished your work. (Müller 130)

Unlike the Young Comrade in Brecht's *The Measures Taken*, A refuses to accept death but willingly goes to the wall.

Structurally, *Mauser* is noted as a transitional work in Müller's career because it does away with most typical line assignments and character representation in favor of poetic "block" text. Müller began, with *Mauser*, to do away with clear positionality, opting instead to use multiple actors to present two or more contradictory positions. In his notes to *Mauser* Müller suggests, "Performance for an audience is possible if the Chorus part is read by one group of spectators and the part of the First Player by another group of spectators. The proposed distribution of the text is variable, the mode and degree of variants a political choice that has to be made in each individual case" (Müller, *Battle* 133). Müller then notes possible ways that the text may be staged:

> All Chorus performers, at once or one after another, perform the part of the First Performer, the First Performer speaks certain segments of the Chorus' speeches while A1 performs his role. No performer can assume another's role all the time. Experiences are only transmitted by and in a collective; the training of the (individual) capacity to make experiences is a function of the performance. A member of the Chorus who, after his killing, will again assume his place in the Chorus plays the Second Performer (listed as B). (133)

Müller's text creates a true collective experience in the theatre, as the positional duality of A, B, and the Chorus are portrayed by all performers. Each of the performers embodies both sides of the argument. All play the roles of judge, jury, and accused. As Jonathan Kalb notes in *The Theatre of Heiner Müller,* "Part of what is so disturbing about *Mauser* is the absence of a fully human, heroic center on which audiences may fix their sympathies" (54). In fact, given the "all inclusive" nature of the text, and the alienating nature of the discourse, audiences may realize that in *Mauser* they too are capable of the type of Orwellian doublespeak that Müller criticizes. With *Mauser* Müller surpasses the border that separates life from theatre—the frame of individual character representation.

Works Cited

Brecht, Bertolt. *Brecht on Theatre.* Trans. and ed. John Willett. London: Methuen, 1964.

———. *The Measures Taken and Other Lehrstücke.* London: Methuen, 1989.

Doe, Andrew E. "Brecht's Lehrstücke: Propaganda Failures." *Educational Theatre Journal* 14 (1962): 289–96.

Huettich, H. G. *Theatre in the Planned Society: Contemporary Theatre in the German Democratic Republic.* Chapel Hill: University of North Carolina Press, 1978.

Kalb, Jonathan. *The Theatre of Heiner Müller.* London: Cambridge University Press, 1998.

Müller, Heiner. *Krieg Ohne Schlacht.* Köln: Kiepenheuer and Witsch, 1992.

———. *The Battle.* New York: PAJ Publications, 1989.

Rouse, John. *Brecht and the West German Theatre.* Ann Arbor: University of Michigan Press, 1989.

Sontheimer, Kurt, and Wilhelm Bleek. *The Government and Politics of East Germany.* London: St. Martin's Press, 1975.

Circulating *Power*

National Theatre as Public Utility in
the Federal Theatre Project

Kurt Eisen

I N December 1938, with FDR's New Deal programs increasingly
under fire by opponents in Congress, Hallie Flanagan appeared before the House Un-American Activities Committee to defend her work
as national director of the Federal Theatre Project. Several key congress-
men were already set to kill her program, including HUAC member
J. Parnell Thomas, who had declared the Federal Theatre nothing more
than "sheer propaganda for the New Deal or Communism" (Bentley 3).

During Flanagan's testimony HUAC chairman Martin Dies took special interest in a play that had achieved critical and financial success
in New York, Seattle, San Francisco, Chicago, and Portland, a Living
Newspaper called *Power,* which advocates the public ownership of electric utilities in general and the Tennessee Valley Authority (TVA) in
particular. Here is a brief excerpt from the Dies-Flanagan exchange:

> [DIES]: What is the objective of the play, what impression is it designed
> to bring in the mind of the audience—the play *Power*—that public own-
> ership is a good thing?
> [FLANAGAN]: I think the first thing the play does is to make you under-
> stand more about power, where it comes from, and how it is evolved, about
> its whole historical use. . . . I think it also does speak highly for the public
> ownership of power.
> [DIES]: And if someone came with a play showing the public ownership
> of all the property in the United States, and it was a good play, you would
> also exhibit that, would you not?
> [FLANAGAN]: No, I would not, we would stop with that, because that
> would be recommending the overthrow of the United States Govern-

ment, and I do not want that, gentlemen, whatever some of the witnesses have been saying. (Bentley 39–41)

Flanagan knew that Dies was pushing her to confirm charges of pervasive communism in the Federal Theatre Project. Dies hoped to prove that communist ideology was at the heart of the Federal Theatre, informing its most distinctive stage genre, the Living Newspaper, especially such box-office successes as *One Third of a Nation,* which portrayed the nation's housing crisis, and *Power.* Flanagan resisted any such admission, but it was clear enough to Dies, Parnell, and other critics of the New Deal's creeping socialism that the ultimate goal of the Federal Theatre Project was to use public funds to do what the privately owned commercial stage could not or would not do. Just as the TVA sought to electrify impoverished rural areas deemed unprofitable by private power companies, the Federal Theatre tried to bring a kind of cultural enfranchisement to areas that had been left outside the circulation of mass culture in the early twentieth century.

Members of the Dies committee wanted, among other things, for Flanagan to betray a desire for a "national" theatre, which they saw as part of a larger plan to nationalize cultural institutions after the manner of the Soviet Union. Flanagan explicitly denied any such goal (Bentley 9), although she strongly believed in the federal government's role in fostering the arts. This essay will examine what kind of theatre Flanagan was working for, especially how her concept of a "federal" theatre paralleled the goals and management philosophy of the TVA and its early leaders, most notably David Lilienthal, a founding TVA director, its third chairman, and its most aggressive proponent of its role as a public utility.

The play's title, *Power,* points beyond the immediate issues of rural electrification and affordable utility rates, suggesting that bringing technology and culture to marginal communities inevitably creates a new measure of political empowerment, threatening capitalism's vested structures of valuation and control. This leads to a further question: Why did the TVA, despite its threat to private ownership, survive the New Deal backlash of the later 1930s, expanding well beyond its initial mandate in later decades, whereas the Federal Theatre Project was summarily axed in the summer of 1939, never to be revived in any comparable form?

It might be said that Flanagan found herself always mediating an ideological split in the Federal Theatre that resembled the decisive early conflict between the TVA's visionary founding chairman Arthur Morgan and his successor, the more pragmatic Lilienthal. Morgan saw the TVA as a great experiment in social engineering that went far beyond flood control and hydroelectricity. He wanted the TVA to take on a wide range of issues, including economic development, education, and racial equality. Unlike Lilienthal, Morgan believed that Americans needed an ethical reeducation away from selfish individualism toward what he would later call "a loyalty to the totality that is greater than their own group and self-interest" (Morgan 182). By contrast, Lilienthal promoted a much more decentralized model of federal involvement, emphasizing local control as the best means of improvement, a concept he introduced as "grass roots administration" in a 1939 speech in Knoxville (Neuse 124). After a high-profile showdown Lilienthal's more pragmatic vision prevailed, and Morgan was out.

Flanagan likewise found herself frequently at odds with more politically aggressive Federal Theatre elements. The Living Newspaper got off to a rocky start in 1935 when its first production, *Ethiopia,* was pulled because the State Department feared damaged relations with Mussolini's Italy, whose recent invasion of Ethiopia was the play's focus. The next year she clashed with director Joseph Losey over *Injunction Granted,* a staunchly prolabor Living Newspaper about the history of American unions and labor law, even including American Communist Party leader Earl Browder onstage briefly as a character. Flanagan fought to keep the politics of the Living Newspaper Unit within the range of progressive New Deal liberalism. As Federal Theatre scholar Lorraine Brown observes, by the time *Power* opened in 1937 Losey was gone and Flanagan had managed to shift the Living Newspaper from a potentially radical to a reformist enterprise (Brown xv).

Although its playwright Arthur Arent, and indeed Flanagan herself, still envisioned the Living Newspaper as a force for social reform, the theme of electrification in *Power* brought its politics of inclusion much closer to the prevailing national faith in progress through technology, a belief shared by conservative defenders of capitalism and Popular Front leftists. Although the TVA itself was by no means universally embraced—certainly not by the private power companies caricatured in *Power*—it did offer a model of nonradical, communitarian New Deal reform that approximated Flanagan's idea of a nationwide theatre movement that would be progressive but not partisan. Theatre, she believed, like electrification and other forms of technological progress, could be conceived as a universal good that transcended political disagreement.

This pushed the Federal Theatre beyond its initial mandate of supplying jobs to out-of-work theatre professionals under the auspices of the Works Progress Administration. As Flanagan explains in *Arena,* she hoped "to extend the boundaries of theatre-going, to create a vigorous new audience, to make the theatre of value to more people" (43). Although the Federal Theatre promoted a full range of dramatic performance, including children's theatre, foreign-language and radio plays, puppetry, vaudeville, pageants, and circuses, Flanagan saw each unit as rooted in its particular locale, promoting scripts and performance styles suited to local communities and traditions. She called it a "federation of theatres" (23), as opposed to a national theatre that imposed its centralized cultural agenda from Washington or New York. Where the needed theatre professionals were in short supply, as in the rural South, they were brought in from the Northeast and Midwest. But in principle their productions were to stay close to regional concerns, were supervised by regional administrators, and strove, as Flanagan put it, to "get plays out of the people themselves" (91). In any case it was plain from the start that Flanagan would not be content with creating jobs for unemployed actors and stagehands or with merely reinforcing the regional status quo. As she told Federal Theatre staffers in 1935, "The theatre must become conscious of the implications of the changing social order, or the changing social order will ignore, and rightly, the implications of the theatre" (46).

The Living Newspaper suited Flanagan's ideals by addressing current local issues in a progressive way. In his influential study of 1930s "documentary expression," William Stott (who begins his book with an homage to Flanagan's 1931 docudrama about impoverished southern farmers, *Can You Hear Their Voices?*) identifies a belief implicit in social documentary: the facts it depicts can be altered (Stott 25). The very act of documenting a social problem—whether in a photograph, an essay, or a script for the stage—presents that problem as a human construct and, therefore, as capable of a human solution. In the South, which Flanagan saw as the Federal Theatre's biggest challenge because of its "rich dramatic material" along with its lack of theatre professionals, she encountered a regionalism that did not embrace social documentary as part of its own culture (Flanagan 81). For this reason *Power,* although it depicts the TVA and features Tennesseans in several scenes, was not staged in the South. Its West Coast productions were partly intended to stir up interest in public power companies similar to TVA, such as the one proposed on the Columbia River in the Northwest (Neuse 128).

Southern Agrarian intellectuals certainly resisted any artificially accelerated form of cultural development in the 1930s, with writers such as Donald Davidson and John Crowe Ransom deeply suspicious of the "machine economy" promoted by TVA electricity. In a 1934 essay, "The

Aesthetic of Regionalism," Ransom laments the increasing urbanization of America and its growing emphasis on consumerism as the highest measure of earthly good (306). By identifying its recurring everyman hero as "Consumer," *Power* seems to bear out Ransom's fear that
the TVA—and by implication New Deal cultural enterprises such as the
Federal Theatre—shared a vision of remaking all of America according
to an industrial-consumerist model, a nationalist agenda in regionalist
clothing.

In one telling sequence near the end of act 1, in scene 15-A, set some-
where in the Tennessee Valley near Chattanooga, a farmer and his wife
wrangle over whether they should fight for access to electricity. The
farmer laments that no one can fight the power company if it refuses to
build lines into the backcountry, but his spunky wife is less submissive:
"Who says you can't go up there and raise holy blazes until they give
'em to you! Tell 'em you're an American citizen! Tell 'em you're sick
and tired of lookin' at fans and heaters and vacuums and dish-washin'
machines in catalogues, that you'd like to use 'em for a change!" In a
significant flourish, she adds, "What the hell do you think Andy Jackson
you're always talkin' about would do in a case like this?" (Arent 63).
In the next scene (15-B) a "City Man" and his wife discuss their inflated
electric bills, the man referring to himself as "one little consumer" who,
like the farmer, cannot possibly fight the monolithic utility company.
Again the wife cajoles her milquetoast husband to fight for his American
birthright, with a clinching point that would make even Andy Jackson
proud: "And tell 'em . . . you'll be damned if you'll give up listening to
those football games on Saturday afternoon!" (Arent 65).

This shift from "Farmer" to "City Man" with an increasing sense of
enfranchisement as a consumer dramatizes precisely the sort of thing
Ransom feared. Moreover, it reflects the situation of the Federal Theatre itself: with rural units losing money and city theatres doing com-
paratively well (Witham 211), the implicit message was that life is im-
proved insofar as it moves closer to the amenities of urban culture. The
reference to football on the radio also points to the electronic mass
culture that would break down the distinctiveness of regional cultures
in the decades to follow.

In his revealing study of the Federal Theatre in the Midwest, Paul
Sporn notes the two differing brands of regionalism that often clashed
in 1930s America: a progressive regionalism, something like Flanagan's
vision of the Federal Theatre's mission, and its conservative counter-
part, exemplified by southern Agrarians like Ransom (50–56). Both were
opposed to greedy industrialists, but conservative regionalism favored
a more organic, "natural" development of cultural tradition and prac-

tice. To accelerate the growth of theatrical performance, even in works that incorporated local concerns, themes, and performance modes, was to take a social-engineering approach to regional culture.

Flanagan's progressive regionalism, at least with respect to the South, is perhaps best revealed in her assessment of the play *Altars of Steel,* which she called "our most important southern production" (Flanagan 88). Written by a Birmingham author but directed by a New Yorker, the play focuses on the steel industry in Alabama and more generally on the debilitating effect of trade tariffs on southern industrial development. Some saw in it a necessary dose of truth, whereas others decried it as "dangerous propaganda" that betrayed the South's genteel traditions and agrarian ideals (Flanagan 88–89).

In effect, Flanagan found herself and her vision for the Federal Theatre caught between these conflicting versions of regionalism, tradition clashing with change. She shared the approach that Lilienthal employed in propagating the TVA, and both were in effect trying to develop new consumers and markets by extending the boundaries of cultural and economic empowerment. Lilienthal's concept of decentralized regional control within the TVA, although highly successful, was in fact more like a screen, "a protective ideology" for what was in fact a centralized organization (Neuse 140). The Agrarian writer Donald Davidson offered this assessment of Lilienthal's TVA: "They had no trouble in transferring to a vast, modern, technological, socialistic undertaking the cheery motivations of the nonsocialistic, untechnological past. They were careful not to say that the people were 'too damned dumb to understand,' but they knew that if folks received cheap electric current and certain other popular improvements, no ugly questions would be asked" (Davidson 325). On the other hand, Living Newspapers such as *Power* were built on asking questions, sometimes ugly ones. *Power* concludes in fact with a large question mark projected on a scrim, signifying a case pending before the U.S. Supreme Court to decide the TVA's constitutionality (Arent 91).

The TVA as public utility managed to survive charges of creeping socialism because it proved more successful at representing itself as a force for democracy rooted in its region. Lilienthal's rhetorical and political skills deserve much of the credit. Certainly the need for hydroelectric power to supply the Manhattan Project at Oak Ridge in the early 1940s was also a big help. As it happens, the only Federal Theatre activities in Tennessee that Flanagan records in *Arena* were benefit shows for flood relief in Knoxville in 1937 (Flanagan 431). Although she was just as sincere in promoting cultural regionalism as Lilienthal was in promoting industrial regionalism, a primarily cultural enterprise such as theatre, when initiated from outside a region, perhaps inevitably highlights social divisions and upsets the status quo. Moreover, Agrarian intellectuals in the South were not apt to embrace a New Deal cultural project when they were struggling to prevent their own ideals from being swallowed up by the TVA and other modernizing forces. They were certainly not likely to encourage the sort of egalitarian, integrationist labor practices that were barely tolerated in the TVA and, as Barry Witham has shown, also prevailed in Federal Theatre units (203). Flanagan may have genuinely believed that theatre could somehow be progressive without being "political," but, Agrarian intellectuals aside, Americans have been much more willing to view technological change as essentially apolitical. In any case the four-year experiment of the Federal Theatre Project from 1935 to 1939 showed, briefly, what new kinds of cultural power might be generated when a determined theatre artist has the wherewithal to oversee a network of regional theatres as if they belonged to the people.

Works Cited

Arent, Arthur. *Power.* In *Federal Theatre Plays.* New York: Random House, 1938. Reprint, New York: Da Capo, 1973.

Bentley, Eric, ed. *Thirty Years of Treason.* New York: Viking, 1971.

Brown, Lorraine, ed. Liberty Deferred *and Other Living Newspapers of the 1930s.* Fairfax: George Mason University Press, 1989.

Davidson, Donald. *The New River: Civil War to TVA.* Vol. 2 of *The Tennessee.* New York: Rinehart, 1948. Reprint, Nashville: Sanders, 1992.

Flanagan, Hallie. *Arena: The History of the Federal Theatre.* New York: Duell, Sloan, and Pearce, 1940. Reprint, New York: Benjamin Blom, 1965.

Morgan, Arthur E. *The Making of the TVA.* Buffalo: Prometheus, 1974.

Neuse, Steven M. *David E. Lilienthal: The Making of an American Liberal.* Knoxville: University of Tennessee Press, 1996.

Ransom, John Crowe. "The Aesthetic of Regionalism." *American Review* 2 (1934): 290–310.

Sporn, Paul. *Against Itself: The Federal Theatre and Writers' Projects in the Midwest.* Detroit: Wayne State University Press, 1995.

Stott, William. *Documentary Expression and Thirties America.* New York: Oxford University Press, 1973.

Witham, Barry. "The Economic Structure of the Federal Theatre Project." In *The American Stage: Social and Economic Issues from the Colonial Period to the Present,* ed. Ron Engle and Tice L. Miller, pp. 200–214. Cambridge: Cambridge University Press, 1993.

The Finger in the Eye

Politics and Literature in
the Theatre of Dario Fo

James Fisher

Art is above all ideology!

—Dario Fo, *Tricks of the Trade*

Giving the [Nobel] prize to someone who is also the author of question-
able works is beyond all imagination.

—The Vatican, quoted in Bohlen

Dario Fo won the Nobel Prize! For a brief moment, the world becomes
a carnival stage; the Fo Effect.

—Tony Kushner

I TALIAN DRAMA in the twentieth century is enveloped by the works
of two Nobel Prize–winning playwrights, Luigi Pirandello (1934)
and Dario Fo (1997). Despite their differences in style and substance,
Pirandello and Fo are similar in their uses of the satiric power of humor
and in the influences they drew on from stage traditions—most particularly the commedia dell'arte. Pirandello's Nobel Prize honored a
self-consciously literary dramatist, but Fo's acknowledgment is, on the
face of it, a much more radical choice. He himself does not think of
his plays as literary; they are "throwaway" farces intended to address
immediate political and social concerns in direct communion with an
audience living with the issues depicted. From a literary standpoint Fo's
plays can be regarded as little more than sketches; they permit him,
frequently as his own leading actor, to improvise and revise—on a daily
basis if necessary—in response not only to interaction with his audience
but also to changing currents of news and public opinion.

Fo's selection for the Nobel Prize for literature brought forth a loud
chorus of nay-sayers claiming that his plays are not, in fact, *literature*

and that Fo is more *actor* than *dramatist*. Fo would have no argument with that, and although the inherent issues in the connection between actor and playwright are certainly worth exploration, the negative response to Fo's selection seems to have more to do with his left-wing politics and themes, as well as with the powerful targets of his wit. In his Nobel acceptance speech—and with his tongue firmly planted in his cheek—Fo congratulated the selection committee for "an act of courage that borders on provocation" (Fo, "Contra Jogulatores Obloquentes" 4). Various branches of the Italian government—and, indeed, of governing entities throughout the world—multinational corporations and their CEOs, and the Catholic Church have most frequently felt Fo's "finger in the eye"—an expression taken from the title of a cabaret entertainment Fo co-wrote in the 1950s. The Vatican was particularly vehement in its condemnation of Fo's Nobel award because his *Mistero Buffo* (1969), *The Pope and the Witch* (1990), and *The Devil with Boobs* (1997), among others, have comically revised Church doctrine and history. Typically taking the role of the anarchic fool (a character Fo refers to as "the maniac" in *Accidental Death of an Anarchist* [1970]), Fo performs in most of his own plays, which also include *Archangels Don't Play Pinball* (1959), *He Had Two Pistols with White and Black Eyes* (1960), *Seventh: Steal a Bit Less* (1964), *The Lady's Not for Discarding* (1967), *Grand Pantomime* (1968), *Can't Pay? Won't Pay!* (1974), *Trumpets and Raspberries* (1981), *Elizabeth* (1984), *Hellequin, Arlekin, Arlecchino* (1985), and *Johann Padan Discovers America* (1991).

If, as *New York Times* critic Mel Gussow writes of Fo's Nobel Prize, it was "the first time the honor had been given to an actor and clown" (E2), then it is obvious that Fo's selection invites us to reconsider and expand previously understood boundaries between *literature* and *theatre, actor* and *writer*. If Fo's Nobel was meant to sound a legitimizing cord in regard to the worth of the performer's art and to recognize "the contribution of comedy, and, in particular, of political satire" (Gussow E2), the importance of understanding how these areas might be interpreted in light of Fo's work is necessary. Whether or not Fo's selection permanently changes the way the Nobel selection committee views literature and the place of the performing artist—and, in fact, whether any award has any significant meaning—it at least suggests that this august body of cultural legitimacy has an impudent sense of the ridiculous. Playwrights in general have only rarely received the Nobel honor—among those recipients whose work was predominantly in the dramatic vein, only Maeterlinck, Benavente, O'Neill, Shaw, Pirandello, Beckett, and Soyinka stand out. Among others, Yeats and Sartre, who refused the honor, wrote plays but were undoubtedly acknowledged more for their achievements in other literary forms. Also interesting to consider are those towering playwrights of the past hundred or more years who did not win a Nobel: Ibsen, Strindberg, Chekhov, Brecht, Lorca, De Filippo, Williams, Ionesco, Albee, and Miller seem especially egregious omissions—certainly others might be added to this list. With perhaps the exception of Beckett among the prior dramatic winners, all of these writers are "literary" in almost any traditional understanding of the word. Eric Bentley writes that Fo's work is not "on the high level of [Eduardo] De Filippo's" (Bentley 6), and he laments the fact that De Filippo did not win it because, like Fo, he was also thought of more as an actor/director than as a playwright. Bentley's preference is difficult to understand, for although De Filippo's plays certainly hold up as literature in ways that Fo's never will, De Filippo's impact on the social and political fabric of the society of his time is decidedly less than Fo's by any standard of assessment. As D. T. Max writes, Fo "is a believer in truly popular entertainment, having long taken his theatre on the road to bowling alleys, open-air stages and workmen's organizations" (31), and Fo would hardly have thought of himself as primarily a playwright, despite the impressive fact that he has written more than seventy plays. Max suggests that Fo's appeal "resides in this elasticity. It takes courage to reinvent your work, and even more to invite, as Fo does, others to reinvent it for you. There's a sublime egolessness to his approach" (31). Tony Kushner, Pulitzer Prize–winning author of *Angels in America,* and no stranger to the sort of controversies that have swirled about Fo's plays or the left-wing politics behind them, writes that popular entertainers have typically been seen as "the wrong sort of people to let into the Club of Perfectly Twizzled Sentences and Imperishable Ideas, not contenders for the Tolstoyan Mantle almost all novelists seem to assume they'll inherit if they reach middle age with three books still in print" (5). Kushner argues that playwrights use words in "rougher and more exigent" ways, and when dramatists can hold an audience with works of depth and complexity, "the accomplishment is worth lauding, in spite of the vexed befuddlement of the guardians of 'literary value'" (5). Kushner also stresses that doubters are usually most shrill when the writer is overtly political, or, as he puts it, "genuinely brave and useful," and that the "prize augments and amplifies Fo's dangerous silliness; Fo in return graciously augments and amplifies the prize's essential silliness. Both in the process are ennobled. I for one can't wait to see the pictures of Fo in Stockholm. The women who come to escort him to the king should in his honor wear Roman candles atop their heads" (4–5).

How, then, to judge the merits of Fo's dangerous silliness? Certainly one question in understanding literature in relation to Fo is whether a literary work is something that is permanently fixed in time. This is certainly not the case with Fo's work, although scripts of many of his plays are in print—especially since he was awarded the Nobel Prize. Works of most prior Nobel winners, even those long forgotten, are there to be read and performed much as they would have been at the time they were first written or at the time their authors were awarded the prize. Will the scripts for Fo's plays stand such a test of time? Is Fo's work, by its very nature, too topical, too temporal, too disposable? Must it be seen in performance with an inspired clown such as Fo?

These questions also raise others of significance in understanding Fo's achievements. His use of the comic form for Marxist-inspired political ends, drawing on the example of the medieval and Renaissance jester, allows Fo the opportunity of turning language upside down by essentially inventing a language all his own—*grammelot*—which he describes as a "method of producing the semblance of a given language without adopting real or identifiable words from that language" (Fo, *Tricks of the Trade* 34). For those in the English-speaking world Fo's work can only be seen in translation—and most frequently *adapted* translations—and, as such, the grammelot is difficult to translate; thus another level of difficulty emerges in attempting to understand his works as literature in the permanent sense.

Defining literature presents many dilemmas because there are centuries of diverse definitions to consider. It seems that what is literary depends to a large extent on what is generally accepted as literature in any time and place. Standard reference definitions of literature describe it variously, but as J. A. Cuddon writes in *The Penguin Dictionary of Literary Terms and Literary Theory,* it is a "vague term which usually denotes works which belong to the major genres: epic, drama, lyric, novel, short story, ode"; Cuddon adds that "there are many works which cannot be classified in the main literary genres which nevertheless may be regarded as literature by virtue of the excellence of their writing, their originality and their general aesthetic and artistic merits" (505–6). Certainly these last generalities would admit Fo's plays to the literary realm.

In *Theory of Literature* René Wellek and Austin Warren distinguish between *literature* and *literary study,* noting that "one is creative, an art; the other, if not precisely a science, is a species of knowledge or of learning," but they conclude that although it is possible to consider anything in print as literature, a distinction needs to be made between "everyday and literary language" (15, 23). In literature, as Wellek and Warren stress, the "reference is to a world of fiction, of imagination"

(25), but literature surely is also by nature either true or false (real or fictive) and makes use of language in peculiar and particular ways. Wellek and Warren discuss the need for the imposition of "an order, an organization, a unity of its material" in a work of literature, and they conclude that it is "best to consider as literature only works in which the aesthetic function is dominant" (25).

Marxist cultural historian Raymond Williams, writing in *Keywords. A Vocabulary of Culture and Society,* notes the distinctions often drawn between literature and drama on the grounds that drama "is a form primarily written for spoken performance (though often also to be read)" (184). The only clear distinction Williams is able to make between literature and drama is that drama is "writing for speech" (186), whereas literature excludes speaking of the written words.

Standard literary definitions do not accommodate Fo except in the most general way, and there is an uneasiness about where to place any kind of drama, although most include it as a genre within the literary realm. Fo's use of nonliterary language—and the language of his own invention—and improvisatory techniques suggests that his work is, like commedia dell'arte, a consciously nonliterary form of drama that emphasizes the skill of the actor. Commedia actors transformed human folly and vice into incisive satire as they created a play before the audience's eyes using only a simple scenario cruder in construction than even the sketchiest of Fo's plays. Commedia's reign on European stages for more than two hundred years, from the early sixteenth through the late eighteenth centuries, influenced theatrical practice in established and emerging cultures and provided a consciously nonliterary model for the stage. At the same time, commedia also provided characters, plots, and comic business as inspiration for literary plays written during the Renaissance and well into the eighteenth century and beyond. Here the literary drama is heavily indebted to commedia as Fo is indebted to it. Perhaps Fo's plays and characters may prove similarly fruitful for more traditional literary writers in the future. Fo's plays, like commedia, offer what might be described as a new form of literary endeavor—theatrical works of ritualized carnival, a popular street theatre that serves as communal self-examination but also as a political instrument through its inherent satire and mockery of the powerful that can remain up-to-the-minute in its direct contact with events as they unfold. Commedia's triumph was that this seemingly casual and lowly form of street theatre became a kind of lingua franca of the imagination, connecting cultures, artists, and literary writers throughout Europe. Like the best and rarest forms of theatre, commedia proved to be universally malleable and national, adapting in each country to the needs of that culture's artists and audiences. This is certainly true of at least some of Fo's plays, but it does not resolve questions about their merit as literature.

A traditional literary work is presumed to be carefully constructed and to adhere to an established form. The informality of Fo's plays should by no means suggest that they are casually created; they are, in fact, the result of considerable research and study. Fo is an expert on the traditions of the stage fool in his many guises and on the long and complex history of the commedia, as well as on other forms of popular street theatre. Through study he rediscovered and was most impressed by the history and techniques of medieval Italian street entertainers (*giullare*) and their equivalents in other regions. Commedia belonged first and foremost to the Italians, and its spirit is alive today in its land of origin; it also remains Italy's most potent calling card on the international stage. Fo has also drawn on his interests in circus, puppetry, carnival, music halls, *teatro grottesco*, and Punch and Judy. He does not accept commedia as a generic, unified form but instead articulates it as a form comprising distinctly variant styles. He acknowledges that there is "a *part* of the *Commedia dell'Arte*, which I have taken and used," but he stresses that many original commedia troupes, such as the Gelosi, and others like them, were "generally conservative, and often downright reactionary in content" (*Dario Fo and Franca Rame* 8), as a result of the patronage they accepted from Italian nobility. He suggests that the great commedia troupes of most use to him were "a bit like those football teams nowadays that are owned by big industrialists" (*Dario Fo and Franca Rame* 8). Fo's plays, again, like sporting events, are not static or permanently fixed, and even his best known, most produced works have undergone continual revisions to keep them attuned to the currents of political change. To recreate commedia, he insists, "you have to decide which political line, which cultural direction you are going to take as the basis for your work" (*Dario Fo and Franca Rame* 8).

Having mastered commedia techniques, Fo studied the works of playwrights with whom he felt an affinity, including Plautus, Shakespeare, Molière, Pirandello, and De Filippo, but never with the intention of creating a polished work of dramatic literature. In fact, Fo believes that such works are antithetical to his kind of drama: "Theatre has nothing to do with literature, even when, by fair means or foul, people go out of their way to force it into line. . . . However paradoxical it may seem, a genuine work of theatre should not at all appear a great pleasure when read: its worth should only become apparent on the stage" (Fo, *Tricks of the Trade* 183). In his Nobel speech Fo reached back to the theatrical past for an even stronger influence than the literary dramatists, acknowledging Angelo Beolco—Ruzzante ("The Joker")—whom he calls "the true father of *commedia dell'arte*" (Fo, "Contra Jogulatores Obloquentes" 4). Beolco's model encouraged Fo to "free myself from conventional literary writing and to express myself with words you can chew, with unusual sounds, with various techniques of rhythm and breathing, even with the rambling nonsense speech of the grammelot" (Fo, "Contra Jogulatores Obloquentes" 4). Fo believes that the free-lance commedia performers, who had a significant and immediate influence on the life of the general populace during the Renaissance, are worthy of emulation. They were "professionals, who didn't frequent the courts and nobility, but worked in taverns, worked in town squares, worked in far lowlier circumstances" (Fo, *Tricks of the Trade* 183).

What connects Fo to commedia and, at the same time, makes him something more than a mere emulator of a past form is that he is a thoroughly engaged citizen of his society, even if some critics have suggested that his far-left political persuasions place him too far out on the fringe. Margaret Spillane writes that Fo's style "avoids denunciation in favor of a rope-a-dope: Give the pontiff or banker or commissar center stage, let him preen and posture and punch the air until he's pooped, then deck him" (6). Fo himself says simply, "I always criticize all the people who are in charge of any country" (Lyman A8), and his choice of inspirations reflects that goal.

The vehicle for Fo's satire is the central figure of each of his plays—himself, both as actor and character. Fo made a permanent break with the conventional bourgeois stage in the early 1960s, announcing his wish to become a minstrel of the proletariat. From that point on he mingled Marxist agitprop with performance techniques drawn from the "lyrical rag-and-bone men who wore masks" (Fo, *Tricks of the Trade* 7) of medieval and Renaissance forms of street theatre. "I did not come into theatre with any ambition to play Hamlet, but with the aspiration to be the red-nosed comic, the clown" (Fo, *Tricks of the Trade* 84), he writes, and his desire to defeat various forms of oppression through a mocking of power, hypocrisy, and "official" lies—both specific and generalized—is set into his belief that overtly political theatre need not be a synonym for either dull or pedantic theatre.

Fo's stage persona is a catalyst who views indignation as a means of catharsis and liberation. Since the early 1970s Fo's plays have been performed throughout Europe and America, and he continues to write and perform in Italy, despite being in his mid-70s. His use of commedia techniques and traditions to create an immediate form of political theatre has stirred controversy because his use of this form, which is often seen as merely lighthearted or decorative by modern audiences, is saturated with his political messages. Fo's goal, since discovering his method and stage persona, has clearly been in sight: Marxism as an ideology with a focus on examining the social, economic, moral, and political plights of the middle and lower classes. His clearly articulated mission is to "advance certain democratic appeals, to form public opinion, to stimulate, to create moments of dialectical conflict" (Carlson 477). The approach is that of an "epic" actor, who sees art as political empowerment, and his work can only be understood as it represents a creative reaction to the most topical social, political, and moral issues. Breaking through the fourth wall of realism, which has dominated so much twentieth-century literary drama—Fo, the playwright and actor, is more the exception than the rule. He uses a text merely as a starting point; in his own particular variation on Brecht Fo's actor is both the character and the actor at all times. The actor is a participatory member of a society recounting social circumstances or injustices and raising questions that may lead an audience to consider solutions to the issues at hand or to raise new questions. To Fo this interaction is more significant than an illusion of naturalism or the preservation of a literary text—his own or anyone else's.

The goal is a spontaneity that a frozen script cannot supply. How can a finished work of dramatic literature ever be fully *in* the present moment except by the happy coincidence that its themes happen to coincide with a current incident? I experienced this myself during a production of Fo's *Accidental Death of an Anarchist* that I directed at Wabash College some years ago. Fo notes that the failure of most productions of his plays outside Italy results from the tendency to turn them into political cartoons featuring exaggerated comic-mafioso stereotypes, draining them of a necessary kind of reality in the dilemmas of the characters while maintaining a presentational performance style. Fo's approach to acting his plays is to keep the production values modest and utilitarian and to make the characters real people caught up in an outrageous situation only slightly exaggerated. This we attempted to do in our production of *Accidental Death of an Anarchist,* a historically based play about the disturbing political reality of police brutality—specifically in a government-sanctioned murder of an accused anarchist—and the resulting disinformation put out by official sources. Fo's script is typical of most of his plays in that he kept it scaled down to allow spontaneity and the alteration of the script on a daily basis as new information emerged. The play was first produced while the real trial of the police officials indicted for the murder was going on, and Fo managed to find lawyers, court officials, and reporters who fed him up-to-date news and copies of unpublished evidence and documents related to the case. Our production opened two days after the Rodney King beating and, in our small way, we accepted Fo's implied invitation to add this news into our production. In such cases the play raises questions and becomes counterinformation, a retelling of the news that asks the audience to respond to shocking truths lurking behind the official account of the situation.

Accidental Death of an Anarchist, like most of Fo's plays, depends on improvisation to maintain a roughness and immediacy in performance. Fo's plays, which he compares to newspaper articles or debates as opposed to literary works, stress an inherent connection between politics and improvisation. *Accidental Death of an Anarchist* is a savagely satiric recounting of events surrounding the actual 1969 bombing of a Milan bank. A self-proclaimed anarchist is arrested for the crime, but within hours he is killed when he falls from a window in police headquarters. The police insist the anarchist's death is a suicide, but inconsistencies in their official account raise serious questions. Fo unleashes his stage fool—a "Maniac"—who insinuates himself into the police station and becomes a one-man carnival employing diverse disguises and subterfuges to expose the distortions and lies of the official story.

Another of his plays that has been frequently produced outside Italy is *Can't Pay? Won't Pay!* This play borrows from traditions of old Neapolitan and Venetian farces that stress that for humanity "the starting point, the fundamental impetus, is hunger" (Mitchell 72). Set in a middle-class apartment, *Can't Pay? Won't Pay!* concerns a housewife, Antonia, who suffers a variety of economic problems. She is involved in a looting incident at a neighborhood market, and it eventually becomes clear to Antonia, and, as Fo intends, to the audience, that her attempt to solve her problems turns into "a need to work collectively, to get organised and fight together—not just for survival, but to live in a world where there are less brightly-lit shop windows, less motorways, and no government corruption, no thieves—the real thieves, the big fish, that is—and where there is justice, justice for all" (Mitchell 73).

In another Fo play, *Elizabeth,* Fo's comic persona switches gender in an attempt to understand and express centuries of oppression faced by women. The fool plays an outrageous "Lady-in-Waiting" to Queen Elizabeth I, who has recently attended a performance of Shakespeare's newest play, *Hamlet,* and considers it a transsexual satire depicting her as an indecisive leader. The queen is actually a ruthless tyrant, and Fo's fool in drag struggles to remain faithful to the queen's womanhood in a male-dominated culture, while also defying her political tyranny. In *The Devil with Boobs,* another commedia-inspired play Fo presented not long before winning the Nobel Prize, he features a typical array of modern stock characters (judge, cardinal, servant, prostitute) to present an assault on the hypocrisies of the wealthy.

Also among Fo's later plays, *Hellequin, Arlekin, Arlecchino* brings him full circle, returning him to his commedia origins. Combining aspects of the *giullare*, Brechtian alienation techniques, and elements of traditional commedia, he includes a prologue outlining the significance of commedia, underscoring its fundamental place in social satire and political activism. As with his earlier works, *Hellequin, Arlekin, Arlecchino* provides Fo with a platform for his satire of prominent figures and issues in contemporary politics. As an actor Fo is, of course, a sophisticated pantomimist but completely disassociated from the familiar white-faced mime. Grotesque and vulgar, his performances have a directness and relevance to contemporary issues a traditional mime avoids. In *Hellequin, Arlekin, Arlecchino* Fo recreated one of his most emblematic pantomimes, based on a traditional *commedia lazzi*. In it his Arlecchino drinks a love potion, causing his penis to grow larger than the rest of him. He then goes through a hilarious array of subterfuges to hide the offending organ, including disguising it as a baby. When a group of village women come by and see him with the "baby," their cooing and petting over it trigger a hilarious kaleidoscope of reactions, suggesting both the character's erotic joy and his fear of discovery. Here, as in most improvisatory situations, the actor is a playwright or, at least, an active commentator on the situation being portrayed. Beyond this bawdy situation, the play focuses on the historical commedia character as an assailant of oppressions; and for Fo this character, and his others based on it, are like Brecht's. They are not acted but represented, with the emphasis placed on the particular situations and ideas that the character articulates. Fo acts in the third person, as in Brecht's epic style, serving as "a 'call boy' who represents the character to the audience, props it up or humiliates it, reports it or condemns it, hates it or loves it, as the case requires" (Fo, "Some Aspects of Popular Theatre" 136).

At this point it is perhaps best to abandon concern for whether Fo's plays are "literary." For Fo the most important issue is that a play must forever remain open to change and continuing response to topical events to be effectively political. *Literature* and *language, character* and *form* are all subservient to *politics*. As previously indicated, Fo's most representative works are grotesque farcical documentaries satirizing governmental and industrial corruption and the resultant problems of survival for the middle and lower classes. It is not surprising, then, that Fo's stage persona emerges as a blasphemous voice of the people, an alter ego for the masses who operate both within the play and outside it. His plays call for radical social change and nonviolent revolution, featuring a profaneness and outrageousness typical, in Fo's mind, of the liberating role of the improvisatory actors of commedia. He envisions theatrical art as political empowerment and abandons stage naturalism and, like Brecht, uses nonrealistic techniques to rid his actors of what he regards as the colorless routine and fraudulent rhetorical exaggeration likely to be found in traditional literary drama. More important, Fo's work dramatizes Brecht's notion that satire, which Fo believes reaches the audience at the deepest level of its intelligence, exists to make people conscious of what Fo calls political truth.

The Marxist content of Fo's plays creates periodic international controversy, with the Nobel Prize only the most recent, highly publicized episode. His life has been threatened by those opposing his political views; there have been bomb threats at places he has performed; Franca Rame, his wife and frequent collaborator, suffered a brutal kidnapping and rape by right-wing thugs; and Fo has occasionally been an unwelcome visitor in several nations, including the United States during the Reagan years. Despite this, Fo has continued to confront the most topical and unsettling issues, recognizing that such an approach exacts a heavy personal price. The end must be that "[c]lowns, like minstrels and 'comics' always deal with the same problem—hunger, be it hunger for food, for sex, or even for dignity, for identity, for power. The problem they invariably pose is—who's in command, who's the boss?" (Fo, *Tricks of the Trade* 172). In his response to Fo's winning of the Nobel Prize, Tony Kushner condemns the view that Fo's work is "too political" for such acknowledgment:

> *Isn't* literature inescapably political? Are there still people—I mean intelligent, progressive people—out there arguing for an aesthetics external to ideology and history? Who *still* believes there's something called "a tragic sense of life," as [Salman] Rushdie puts it, distinct and discernible from the tragedies we concoct and inflict on one another? Who *still* believes that our encounters with the mysteries inherent in being alive and always dying on this earth *aren't* shaped and inflected by the political? (Kushner 5)

Fo believes that widespread ignorance and apathy about various political injustices—both within his own country and internationally—are the wellspring of more injustice. In his Nobel speech he talks of being surprised by how uninformed the younger generation is—perhaps not surprising to those of us who teach the young—although Fo criticizes educators, as well, who, he believes, are equally uninformed and apathetic. In his attempts to teach an audience, the traditions of history, religion, literature, and the stage coalesce.

This is perhaps best exemplified in Fo's masterwork, *Mistero Buffo,* a collection of myths and stories culled from the tales and traditions of medieval jesters. One episode involves a peasant who is so hungry that he is forced to cannibalize his own body—thus man's survival and destruction become one and the same. In another episode Fo mythologizes the birth of the fool character. A poor peasant is brutalized by the local lord and subsequently loses his farm and family. Despondent, he is about to commit suicide when Jesus Christ arrives to give the inarticulate peasant the power of speech so that he might "speak out against bosses, and crush them, so that others can understand and learn, so that others can laugh at them and make fun of them, because it is only with laughter that the bosses will be destroyed." With a kiss on the peasant's mouth Christ accomplishes the transformation, and the fool as a political activist is born. He rushes into the street, and his speech serves as the best possible definition of Fo's ultimate mission: "I am going to joust with the lord of the land, for he is a great balloon, and I am going to burst him with the sharpness of my tongue. I shall tell you everything, how things come and go, and how it is not God who steals! It is those who steal and go unpunished . . . it is those who make big books of laws. . . . They are the ones . . . and we must speak out, speak out" (Fo, *Mistero Buffo* 46–54).

The guiding principle of Fo's approach to the stage is his deeply felt belief that theatre is not isolated from the society that produces it: "A theater, a literature, an artistic expression that does not speak for its own time has no relevance" (Fo, "Contra Jogulatores Obloquentes" 4), he suggests, and he believes that the connection between politics and the nonliterary, improvisatory form of theatre is total, for this choice is "already a political one—because improvisational theatre is never finished, never a closed case, always open-ended" (D'Aponte 537). Fo's effective reliance on satire—whether literary or not—to promote his political beliefs is his highly individual modus operandi, for it is his belief that "[n]othing gets down as deeply into the mind and intelligence as satire. . . . The end of satire is the first alarm bell signaling the end of real democracy" (Fo, "Dialogue with an Audience" 15).

Works Cited

Bentley, Eric. "Of Henrik Pontoppidan and Other Literary Laureates." *New York Times,* 19 October 1997, p. 6.

Bohlen, Celestine. "Italy's Barbed Political Jester, Dario Fo, Wins Nobel Prize." *New York Times,* 10 October 1997, pp. A1, A8.

Carlson, Marvin. *Theories of the Theatre.* Ithaca: Cornell University Press, 1984.

Cuddon, J. A. *The Penguin Dictionary of Literary Terms and Literary Theory.* New York: Penguin, 1976.

D'Aponte, Mimi. "From Italian Roots to American Relevance: The Remarkable Theatre of Dario Fo." *Modern Drama* 32 (December 1989): 532–44.

Dario Fo and Franca Rame Theatre Workshop at Riverside Studios, London. April 28th, May 5th, 12th, 13th and 19th, 1983. London: Red Notes, 1983.

Fo, Dario. "Contra Jogulatores Obloquentes." *World Literature Today* 72.1 (winter 1998): 4–8.

———. "Dialogue with an Audience." *Theatre Quarterly* 9.35 (autumn 1979): 11–16.

———. *Mistero Buffo.* Trans. Ed Emery. Ed. Stuart Hood. London: Methuen Drama, 1988.

———. "Some Aspects of Popular Theatre." *New Theatre Quarterly* 1 (May 1985): 131–37.

———. *The Tricks of the Trade.* Trans. Joe Farrell. Ed. Stuart Hood. London: Methuen Drama, 1991.

Gussow, Mel. "The Not-So-Accidental Recognition of an Anarchist." *New York Times,* 15 October 1997, p. E2.

Kushner, Tony. "Fo's Last Laugh—I." *The Nation,* 3 November 1997, pp. 4–5.

Lyman, Rick. "Using Puns and Pratfalls to Lob Satirical Grenades." *New York Times,* 10 October 1997, A10.

Max, D. T. "The Coronation of a Jester." *New York Times Book Review,* 1 February 1998, p. 31.

Mitchell, Tony. *Dario Fo. The People's Court Jester.* London: Methuen, 1984.

Spillane, Margaret. "Fo's Last Laugh—II." *The Nation,* 3 November 1997, pp. 5–7.

Wellek, René, and Austin Warren. *Theory of Literature.* 3d ed. New York: Harcourt, Brace, and World, 1956.

Williams, Raymond. *Keywords. A Vocabulary of Culture and Society.* Rev. ed. New York: Oxford University Press, 1983.

When Theatre Was a Weapon

(or He Wanted It to Be)

The Theory and Practice of Mordecai Gorelik

Anne Fletcher

ROM HIS BROADWAY DESIGN DEBUT with John Howard Lawson's *Processional* (1925), beyond the publication of *New Theatres for Old* (1940), to the end of his career, Mordecai Gorelik fused theory with practice in portraying his political and artistic philosophies.

Portentous at times, occasionally irascible and dogmatic, Gorelik remained consistent in his philosophy that the purpose of theatre lies in the proactive communication of political ideas.

In the theatrical vanguard of the 1920s and 1930s Mordecai Gorelik was a vital theorist with theatrical vision and political acumen. Of the designers of the day he was the only theorist; of the theorists he was the only designer.

His work between 1925 and 1940 included a number of bona fide "firsts":

(1) *New Theatres for Old* (1940), the first study ever to explore the history of the theatre from the vantage point of stage forms

(2) His assimilation of European scenic practices to the American stage[1]

(3) His conscious use of the popular entertainment idiom in his Broadway designs (initially in the exaggerated vaudeville-burlesque setting for *Processional*, which was produced by the Theatre Guild in 1925)

---

[1]Gorelik studied European staging techniques, and then, coupling them with indigenously American stage conventions, he adapted them to the American stage. In this manner his work differs from that of all other American designers of the 1920s. The designs of Robert Edmond Jones, although innovative and often quite beautiful, remain markedly European in flavor.

(4) His definition of the designer's role in the production process (Gorelik, "I Design" 180–85)

(5) His view of the theatre through the ages as a manifestation of its culture (which predated the "new historicism" by several decades)

(6) His discovery and interpretation for Americans of the theory and practice of Bertolt Brecht, which predated Eric Bentley's[2]

Despite these significant accomplishments, after the publication of *New Theatres for Old* Gorelik was, by and large, ignored. He seems to have lost his chance at lasting fame by designing for plays that fell outside the scope of the accepted dramatic canon, plays that were political and/or production dependent. Even Kingley's Pulitzer Prize–winning *Men in White* has been forgotten by most; of all the scripts for which Gorelik designed, only *Golden Boy* and *All My Sons* are generally included in the dramatic canon.

It would be simple to dismiss Mordecai Gorelik as "stuck" in the 1930s, the decade in which his theories matured and the time when he made his clean break with realism. Indeed, his career-long belief in the theatre's place as a vehicle for social change and as a means for reaching the masses emanated from Gorelik's participation in the political and social theatre of the 1930s.

But after the publication of *New Theatres for Old* in 1940, Mordecai Gorelik lived for another half century! In the 1950s he returned to Broadway; the 1960s found him critiquing two major works on political theatre (Gorelik, "Legacy" 38–43), and two decades later he was condemning absurdism (Gorelik, "Tag Line"; Haddad). Gorelik retired from the "academic theatre" in 1972 and by 1980 was busy peddling the plays he had penned over the course of several decades (Curtiss). In 1988 he published *Toward a Larger Theatre,* a collection of them. When Mordecai Gorelik died in 1990, his theatrical epitaph was still an uncertain one. "I don't know if I will merit 'a place in theatre history.' I should like to think I will be remembered" (Gorelik, letter to author).

The notion that theatre has responsibilities remained with Gorelik for his entire life. The idea that the nature of theatre would evolve to meet the needs of its society was clearly expressed by Gorelik in 1940 as the premise behind *New Theatres for Old:* "Theatre is immortal not because it never dies but because it is always being reborn. When a par-

---

[2]Gorelik first came in contact with Brecht in 1935, when he served not only as designer for *Mother* but as Brecht's translator. His first published article on Brecht was in 1937, five years before Bentley met him (Eric Bentley, *The Brecht Commentaries* [New York: Grove Press, 1981], 15).

ticular theatre comes to an end because it is no longer useful to its audiences, it is replaced by a newer theatre, which takes up the work where its predecessor left off" (Gorelik, *New Theatres* 6). As late as 1988, in *Toward a Larger Theatre,* he declared:

> In the past, world theatre has shown that it can live up to its responsibilities. I believe it will do so again. The escapist mood of our theatre will change—not just because it will be fashionable to do so. It will change because theatre has the task of clarifying. . . . It will change because, as our period's long and terrifying series of world crises mount to a climax, our theatre's playwrights and playgoers will no longer be able to close their eyes and ears. (356)

Gorelik had faith that this perpetual rebirth of the theatre would occur. That he saw the theatre as a means for ameliorating social ills was demonstrated as early as 1922, when he witnessed a strike in Germany. This experience, as documented in his diary, had a profound effect on the man: "Workers had come straight from their factories. They were in overalls. . . . Red flags [were] everywhere, some with symbols of trade and factories on them. . . . [S]ome blazed [*sic*] with white letters: 'Es liebe die Proletariat,' 'Arbeiter der Weld Vereiniget,' 'Hoch die Weld Revolution.'" This "real life drama," coupled with his attendance at the Volksbühne's production of Ernst Toller's *Massemensch,* elicited from Gorelik the telling comment, "I could never again look at theatre as the home of only family problems" (*Toward a Larger Theatre* 4).

Gorelik spent the latter half of the 1920s designing for the New Playwrights, followed by the Group Theatre, the Theatre Collective, and the Theatre Union. He contributed articles to the leftist theatre journals of the day as well. The March 1932 issue of *Workers Theatre,* for example, contained an article by Mordecai Gorelik titled "Scenery: The Visual Attack."

His seminal article, "Theatre Is a Weapon," which appeared in *Theatre Arts Monthly,* summarized the workers' theatre phenomenon in the United States to date (1933) and commented on the cross-pollination of ideas that spread from one theatre company to another.

Gorelik begins this article: "The art of the theatre at any period springs from the social and economic institution of its audience" (420–21). He goes on to discuss typical Broadway fare and its irrelevance to the average worker/audience member. He then chronicles the rise of the workers' theatre from its two original New York units, the Workers Laboratory Theatre and the Prolet-Bühne to the League of Workers Theatres (LOWT), which by 1933 boasted some four-hundred-member organizations (423).

"Theatre Is a Weapon" is critical to an assessment of Gorelik's theory of the theatre for several reasons:

(1) It clearly establishes his belief in the efficacy of theatrical production.

(2) It is written from an undeniably Marxist perspective.

(3) It illustrates Gorelik's proclivity toward depicting the less-attractive side of life as it is rather than depicting the beauty that might be.

Gorelik embraces the workers' credo wholeheartedly:

"Resist war, hunger and fascism, resist anti-semitism and negro segregation, build the international solidarity of labor, defend your fellow workers, defend the Soviet Union, the first workers' government!" This is the cry that rings through the auditoriums of workers' theatres. We are a long way from the Broadway theatre with its leisurely introspection. Workers and farmers facing eviction, strikers on the picket lines, negroes threatened by lynch gangs, have not the time to wait until the commercial theatre, by a vision of abstract beauty, shall teach the world to become a beautiful place to live in. All that in good time, *after the classless society is firmly established.* (424, emphasis mine)

"Theatre Is a Weapon" outlines the cooperative structure of most workers' theatres and describes the limited production elements they had available. Gorelik praises the new theatre companies for their devotion to the education of their participants, offering courses, for example, in theatre history from a Marxist perspective (432). He discusses the leftist theatre dilemma of quality of production versus message, advocating a continued emphasis on improving stage artistry and craft. A start had been made, he believed, with the Theatre Collective's revival of Claire and Paul Sifton's *1931–* (431).

The Siftons' *1931–* is an appropriate piece to view here for a number of reasons:

(1) It exemplifies the spirit of the leftist theatres of the time.

(2) The play's dramaturgical problems illustrate the form-vs.-content dilemma of the workers' theatres.

(3) It was first produced by the Group Theatre, so it demonstrates the interaction between Broadway theatres and the more radical leftist groups.

(4) Mordecai Gorelik was responsible for the sets in both cases.

(5) The Group's failure to keep the play running placed Gorelik at odds with the Group's directors and revealed the difference between Gorelik's level of "commitment" and theirs.

On a grander scale *1931–* and its premiere under the auspices of the Group Theatre represent the philosophical and structural differences between American *political* drama and American *social* drama.

The play is cast in fourteen episodes separated by interludes. It chronicles the disastrous experiences of unemployed Adam, a Great Depression everyman. An altercation with his foreman results in Adam's losing his job. At first he remains cocksure that another lies just around the corner. Reality soon hits. His marriage must be postponed. Humiliated, he roams from potential job site to potential job site, to no avail. He becomes ill and is hospitalized. He has to be carried off a work line when he collapses while he is shoveling snow on a temporary government relief project. He is briefly reunited with his girlfriend but is then forced to press on. Finally, he procures a job sweeping the floor in a coffee shop, working twelve hours a day for twelve dollars a week. In the final scene, by coincidence, Adam's girlfriend walks in. She tells him it is too late for them: she has resorted to prostitution, has contracted a venereal disease, and is very ill. During this scene a mob of communist demonstrators gathers outside the coffee shop. Their volume increases. A policeman ducks inside the coffee shop and calls for reinforcements— machine guns and gas. Adam decides to join the screaming mob. The crowd begins to fight and is gassed. The finale begins on an empty stage; then strains of a song not unlike the "Internationale" are heard in the wings. The play closes as the crowd, Adam now in its midst, marches head on into machine-gun fire.

Leftist critics found the play not resolute enough in its solution to the problem of unemployment; those on the right resented its propagandist elements. On one hand, the play reeks of melodrama, but on the other it exhibits expressionistic, highly stylized episodes and characters. Mordecai Gorelik found himself caught in the midst of a political debate over content and a dramaturgical dispute over form. He had aligned himself (and certainly this would not be the last time) with a text that was pertinent socially but ineffective dramatically.

The Siftons' intent was to write contrapuntally, paralleling the play's structure of alternating interlude and episode with the characters' attitudes toward the revolution. The interludes were intended to provide the perspective of the masses, the solidarity of the crowd. The episodes were meant to illustrate the individual's place in society and the ill effects of a wrongheaded society on him or her.

Both Strasberg's direction and Gorelik's design supported and enhanced the Siftons' goal: "The scenic tableaux he [Strasberg] created for *1931–* were strikingly dramatic, aided by Mordecai Gorelik's remarkable set. The huge corrugated iron walls of the warehouse dominated the stage. Sliding doors within them were raised and lowered to reveal the play's numerous other settings—a park, a Bowery street, a shabby rooming-house interior—but the warehouse itself was always present, an ominous reminder of the mercilous [*sic*] economic forces bearing down on the characters" (Smith 68–69).

With *1931–* the Group Theatre discovered a new audience, which it attempted to accommodate by lowering ticket prices (Smith 71). The interaction between audience and stage was extraordinary: "the balcony was packed every night, while the orchestra remained empty. These viewers were noisier than the average theatre crowd. . . . They followed the action with intensity. . . . On the last night . . . [d]uring the curtain call someone in the balcony called out, 'Long live the Soviet Union!'" (Smith 70). Gorelik saw with *1931–* an opportunity to reach a broader-based audience and to express the proletariat feelings he harbored. Agitated and emphatic, he faced the Group's directors. He questioned the company's motto and insisted that the company should become less commercial, cater to a workers' audience, and try to reach the masses. In retrospect Clurman seems to have paid Gorelik homage as far-sighted, a man ahead of his theatre and ahead of his time:

> Our production of *1931–* . . . made us aware, for the first time, of a new audience. . . . We sensed its stirring, but we did not fully appreciate its value. Mordecai Gorelik . . . tried to call our attention to it—but he had an impatient manner and an extremist approach—or so it seemed to us. It appeared that he wanted us to abandon Broadway at once to reach the audience that couldn't afford Broadway prices. . . . We were impatient with his impatience. (Clurman 72–73)

In the introduction to *Toward a Larger Theatre* Gorelik depicts Harold Clurman's political stance in a humorous light: "Harold Clurman . . . asked me to accompany him to an interview with Sidney Howard. . . . I listened with interest to Clurman's outline of what the group would be. Howard finally asked 'Will your theme be Marxist?' 'We are not going to be restricted by Marxism,' Clurman assured him. To which the dramatist replied, 'Marxism is a pretty roomy philosophy, Harold'" (7).

Group members did become actively involved in the leftist theatre movement—some, as we all know, even in the Communist Party. Many taught classes for the workers' theatres; some directed as well. Virginia Farmer ultimately left the group to direct the Theatre Collective's actor-training program (Smith 127). In 1934–35, when the Collective moved temporarily from producing into the realm of actor exploration, the staff was composed largely of Group Theatre members (Goldstein 29). The Group's props from *1931–* were loaned to the Theatre Collective for its staging of this its inaugural piece (Gorelik, telephone interview).

The Theatre Collective was intended to be a more professional company than the typical worker theatre, and it sought to produce full-length Marxist plays. Its short-lived history is a hazy one at best. Playscripts for most of its pieces do not survive. Participants do not discuss it or reveal in their later writings that they even participated in the Collective at all. A thorough investigation of Gorelik's personal papers discloses very little about the Theatre Collective. He refrained from listing the company on his later resumes, stating simply that it had not been a significant experience in his overall career. He did, however, sanction a study of his work during the "second phase" of communism in America (Gorelik, telephone interview). However cloudy its politics and its production record, the Theatre Collective is important because it constitutes the first firm step on the part of the workers' theatres to move from agitprop to revolutionary realism. It is intriguing in a study of Mordecai Gorelik, for Elia Kazan said of Gorelik and the Collective: "The Theatre Collective won over our cantankerous scene designer, Mordecai Gorelik, who believed the institution to be politically sound" (Kazan 105). At the same time as the Theatre Collective (1932–33), the Theatre Union was developing. It was there that Gorelik would find a political stand and production values most compatible with his own.

Gorelik remained with the Group Theatre, off and on, for nine years, but he spent two years between 1933 and 1940 abroad, studying Russian theatre techniques and continuing his work with the more political theatres.

The 1929 crash of the stock market had precipitated a newfound interest and support for artistic expression that reflected the masses. At the same time, the most radical leftist producing agencies realized that to broaden the scope of their audiences, they needed to adapt their production techniques. The shifting focus of the radical leftist groups coincided with the Group Theatre's increased political awareness, resulting in philosophical and practical cross-pollination. The agitprop of the workers' theatres found more poetic and publicly palatable vehicles in the plays of Clifford Odets.

The year 1935 was a watershed year for those Group members who participated in *Waiting for Lefty*. For Gorelik it represented a line of demarcation—the year he met Bertolt Brecht and turned his back on social realism. His experience designing for Brecht's *Mother* and with the Theatre Union overall led Mordecai Gorelik to opt for "alienation" and "reason" over what he saw as the emotionalism of American social drama.

For the remainder of his life Mordecai Gorelik never designed a set that was *a*political. He may have politicized plays that were not originally political, but he most certainly never *de*politicized a production! His constancy, however, was sometimes difficult to differentiate from his obstinacy.

His consistency is quite remarkable. Although he experimented with various rendering techniques and designed in different styles, Gorelik's philosophy of the theatre did not falter during his long and productive career.

Arthur Miller's recollection of Mordecai Gorelik couples the professional with the personal. He captures the integrity, the grit, and the pigheaded determination of the man: "He was one of those artists sloughed off by American theatre because he was really far too principled. . . . He was also a pain in [the] ass, as you must know" (Arthur Miller, letter to the author).

Works Cited

Clurman, Harold. *The Fervent Years.* New York: DeCapo Press, 1985.

Curtiss, T. Q. "At 80, Gorelik Changes His Act." *Paris International Tribune,* 12–13 July 1980, n.p.

Goldstein, Malcolm. *The Political Stage: American Drama and the Theatre of the Great Depression.* New York: Oxford University Press, 1974.

Gorelik, Mordecai. Diary. 5 July 1922, p. 30.

———. "I Design for the Group Theatre." *Theatre Arts Monthly* 23 (March 1939): 180–86.

———. "The Legacy of the New Deal Theatre." *Drama Survey* 4 (spring 1965): 38–43.

———. Letter to author. 27 November 1987.

———. *New Theatres for Old.* 1940. New York: Samuel French, 1957.

———. "Tag Line." *Dramatics Magazine,* September 1980, n.p.

———. Telephone interview with author. 17 January 1990.

———. "Theatre Is a Weapon." *Theatre Arts Monthly* 18 (January 1933): 420–33.

———. *Toward a Larger Theatre.* Landam, Md.: University Press of America, 1988.

Haddad, Barbara. "Dramatist Raps 'Absurd' Trend." *Denver Post,* 21 April 1965, n.p.

Kazan, Elia. *A Life.* New York: Alfred A. Knopf, 1988.

Miller, Arthur. Letter to author. 16 August 1990.

Smith, Wendy. *Real Life Drama: The Group Theatre and America, 1931–1940.* New York: Alfred A. Knopf, 1990.

Writing the People

Political Theatre on Broadway in Interwar America

Christopher Herr

I N HIS 1849 ESSAY, "The Art-Work of the Future," Richard Wagner outlined his theory of drama, revolutionary not only in form (moving toward what he would call elsewhere the *Gesamtkunstwerk*) but in source. Opposed to traditional bourgeois drama, Wagner's ideal drama originates not from the individual intellect but from the ethical imperative of the "Volk," who call forth their own forms naturally. Further, despite the fact that Wagner was a disappointed revolutionary, his idea of the "Volk" is not determined solely by class, although there is a tendency toward class identification. Especially during times of conflict, he remarks, all individuals seek to ally themselves with the People (Dukore 778). Thus, the Volk is a universally accessible group, naturalized by human need: the romantic ideal of organic form is married to the revolutionary goal of human equality. The Volk is, in Wagner's words, "the epitome of all those men who feel a common and collective Want. To it belong, then, all of those who recognize their individual want as a collective want . . . and therefore spend their whole life's strength upon the stilling of their thus acknowledged common want" (Dukore 778–79). It therefore occupies ethical and aesthetic as well as historical and political territory; the true artwork reflects in form and content the will of the people, rejecting luxury in favor of need.

It is not hard to see how Wagner's valorization of submergence in the common will was appropriated for fascist purposes. Certainly his fervent chauvinism and anti-Semitism have forced a radical questioning of his ostensibly progressive aesthetic. Nevertheless, Wagner's conception of the folk serves as a useful springboard for a discussion of American political theatre, particularly that of the early and mid-twentieth century, given that attempts to define the "people" and the creation of aesthetic forms that would adequately express their ethical-political imperatives are chief concerns of American theatre in the first half of the twentieth century—and beyond. An idea similar to Wagner's concern for the expression of the folk spirit, perhaps spurred by Walt Whitman's call for new forms in his 1870 essay "Democratic Vistas," dominates American theatrical practice between the wars. This idea influences theatre artists from the Little Theatre movement through the Group Theatre and the Theatre Guild, the workers' theatres of the 1930s, and the Federal Theatre Project. It also pervades discussions about the possibilities of film as the new folk art. These theatres, although quite different in goals, methods, and audiences are nevertheless concerned with the same questions: Whose theatre is it? How can theatre find a form that adequately reflects American concerns to an American audience? How can theatre be a tool for social change? And finally: can theatre help to fulfill the promises of democracy, or is it merely a debased form feeding a decadent political system (or worse, an exploitative economic one)? All these theatres answered the questions in their own ways but always with an eye to a particular interpretation of the democratic principles of American politics.

In essence Wagner's idea of the "Art-work of the future" aims to articulate a comparable democratic form. If it is naive, totalizing, and largely unconscious, it nevertheless raises the question of how communal political principles can infuse a theory of drama. Of course, the late romantic, socialist spirit manifest in Wagner's theory has been tempered historically in American theatre by the more conservative tradition of negotiated, majority-rule democracy and especially by the Calvinist-capitalist tradition of fierce individualism. In fact, one can argue that the tension between the individual and the group (not necessarily the state) raises the signature problem of democracy: how to accommodate individual choice in a coalition capable of political action. But as Janelle Reinelt has suggested in "Notes for a Radical Democratic Theater," acceptance of this tension can also be a way to make theatre politically useful in a world unwilling to countenance radical alternatives. If theatre has seemingly lost a common ground for political action, Reinelt argues, then a reinscription of the communal principle is necessary for theatre to again serve as a site for critical examination of democratic principles and practices.

This idea of the communal is far less totalizing and far more open to individual freedom, both in artist and audience, than Wagner's idea of the Volk. Indeed, Reinelt's theory is predicated on an understanding of the inherent differences and conflicts within any idea of community:

she interprets "'crisis' as an enabling state of acute tension . . . often leading to . . . a creative uncertainty" (284). Reinelt goes on to acknowledge that there have been times in American theatre history—the colonial period, specifically—when theatre has been "a place of democratic struggle where antagonisms are aired and considered, and where the voluntary citizenry, the audience, deliberates on matters of state in an aesthetic mode" (289).

Using Reinelt's concept as a radical rethinking of Wagner's basic argument applied to a democracy, I would also suggest that a close look at interwar theatres—especially those with at least one foot in Broadway, such as the Theatre Guild and the Group Theatre—reveals a similar play of political tensions between the individual and the community, between consensus and antagonism, between revolution and reform, between the promises of democracy and the realization of those promises. It is following a well-worn path to note that theatre of interwar America is obsessed with politics; however, analyses of this period often focus on the influence of Marxism and workings of Communist Party politics in American drama. Certainly American theatre had become more explicitly concerned with politics in the post–World War I era, and radical politics had a lasting influence on the theatre, as it did in other arts. I will argue, however, that the forms by which the interest in politics manifested itself are more consistently in keeping with the conception of theatre as an expression of negotiated folk or communal associations —that is, a *democratic* theatre—rather than a specifically Marxist political ideology.

Morgan Himelstein's influential analysis of the communist influence on the theater of the 1930s, although admittedly ferocious in its hatred of communism, has convincingly demonstrated the small foothold communist theory and practice had in the American theatre as a whole. This is not to argue that Marxism had little power in interwar political drama; the evidence is overwhelmingly to the contrary. However, the Marxism practiced in the thirties marched more under the banner of "leftism": even amid the most fervently collectivist efforts of the left in the 1930s, there was still a powerful vestige of democratic individualism. The great struggle, then, in many interwar American theatres— especially those committed to a Broadway audience like the Group and the Guild—is not about how to effect the overthrow of the system but rather how to achieve its true realization, a specific goal of radical democratic theatre. Reinelt quotes Chantal Mouffe: "The problem is not the ideas of modern democracy, but the fact that its political principles are a long way from being implemented, even in those societies that lay claim to them" (Reinelt 284). Or, as Edna says in the quintessential leftist drama of the 1930s, Clifford Odets's *Waiting for Lefty:* "My God, Joe, this world is supposed to be for all of us!" (Odets 10).

Most of the socially conscious interwar theatres, and the playwrights associated with them, saw their mission as finding a proper expression of the folk spirit in American life and drama. Indeed, a great many American playwrights of the period, including many of the most successful— Odets, Maxwell Anderson, Robert E. Sherwood, Elmer Rice, Susan Glaspell, Sidney Howard, John Howard Lawson, Eugene O'Neill—and of the period immediately following, namely Tennessee Williams and Arthur Miller, found great themes in the tension between the ideal of individual success and the power of communal association. Although many of these playwrights express fierce and unrelenting opposition to the system as it operated in the lives of their characters, no one, not even Odets at his most radical, seems unequivocally committed to the overthrow of that system. Even the end of *Waiting for Lefty*, in which Agate Keller calls the taxi drivers "stormbirds of the working class" and exhorts his fellow drivers to action, is more lyrical than revolutionary, dealing as it does with a strike that had taken place a year earlier. One can see, rather, an attempt to give voice to the leftist beliefs that had been creeping into the mainstream since the end of the First World War. Indeed, Odets struggles to find a form for his vision of the folk will, a form that in agitprop was readily available from more radical experiments of the Workers Laboratory Theatre and the Proletbühne. Certainly it is possible to trace through the plays of Odets and these other writers a concern about American politics that intervenes radically in the debate about the successes and failures of the democratic system without necessarily advocating the overthrow of that system.

The tension inherent in Odets's longing for a form to express the ethical-political imperatives of his community mirrors the tension between competing visions of political leftism in the interwar period. Gerald Rabkin and others have argued that, despite the wide influence of Marxism in the arts, communist influence in the United States never had the proletarian appeal it enjoyed in Europe: it was a party of individual inclination rather than strong class identification. Perhaps one of the clearest examples of the struggle, even in the Communist Party, between the individual and the group, is the revolving door of American Party membership during the 1930s. Writers who were attracted to the party because it took a stand against fascism, or fought on the side of the oppressed in Scottsboro and Harlan County, often left when the party made "suggestions" to bring their work more in line with party policy. It took the establishment of the more democratic, antifascist Popular Front in the mid-1930s to permit a form of communism, however attenuated, to gain acceptance in America. In fact, party rigor was tempered in the mid-1930s to the point where "Americanism" became the stated goal for many communist writers (Levine 135).

In part, the Popular Front was an attempt to shore up support for communist ideas in a country politically and temperamentally disinclined toward communism. Nevertheless, between the wars the American disinclination toward the overthrow of the existing system is borne out in the gap between Marxist communist theory and theatrical practice. Ira Levine, in his analysis of left-wing dramatic theory in the United States, has suggested that early leftist theory was often romanticized and ultimately more or less dissociated from theatrical practice. He remarks of early Marxist magazines like *The Masses* and *The Seven Arts* that "while they advocated socialism . . . their leftism was generally more lyrical than practical. A Socialist America represented to them the fulfillment of their aesthetic theory" (13). To be sure, in the early 1930s radical theatres like the WLT and The Proletbühne, as well as individuals like John Howard Lawson in his *Theory and Technique of Playwriting,* made stronger attempts to meld Marxist theory and theatre practice. However, at the same time, the consolidation of a democratic, even utopian, consumer capitalism fueled in part by Roosevelt's New Deal more or less assured the continuation of the current system, however altered. A series of democratically instituted reforms of the capitalist system juxtaposed with leftist plays calling that system into question gives strong evidence of the kind of contradictions that make the theatre of the interwar period a jumble of viewpoints and ideologies influenced but not determined by particular political commitments. It was, in short, a theatre of productive crisis.

Thus it is in the context of a negotiated, tentative, multifarious leftism that the idea of the "Volk" and concept of productive crisis can be best used to examine the concerns central to the political theatres of the time. As I have suggested, these concerns may be expressed most tellingly through the complex interplay between politics and capital, that is, through the development of political theatre on Broadway because Broadway remains the bastion of popular "legitimate" theatre throughout this period, despite the many challenges to its authority.

Of course, any examination of interwar American theatre needs to take into account the tradition of American political theatre from colonial times. As John Gassner has argued, "the socially slanted theatre of the thirties has a long background of journalistic topicality and democratic sentiment" (ix). Gassner's caution implies two important principles. First, the American theatre is by tradition inseparable from conceptions of political structure: the stage mirrors the political arena.

For example, Douglas McDermott has shown that in the 1760s, resistance to the British-controlled theatre was greatest in those cities where the drive for independence from the British was strongest, especially Philadelphia and New York. Theatre regained popularity after the political structures had changed following the revolution (McDermott 8–9). Gassner's second important point is that even if American theatre has always been political, and even if there is a recognizable form of political drama in the post–World War I period directly influenced by Marxism, the idea of "leftism" is more influential than that of strict Marxism: "Leftism . . . was the banner under which one fought *against* fascism and Nazism and *for* human decency and social reforms so soon to be incorporated in the law of the land without commitment to the overthrow of capitalism" (Gassner ix).

For important companies like the Theatre Guild and the Group Theatre, then, the existing structures of capitalist democracy profoundly influenced their use of the political onstage. The Guild, for example, began as an art theatre in an era that saw America testing its political and military strength abroad and attempting to establish a literary nationalism at home. Eschewing an overtly political agenda, the Guild sought to modernize American theatre by bringing in important and experimental European plays and by soliciting a subscription audience, ultimately hoping to establish an American theatre based on European models. The founders of the first incarnation of the Guild, the Washington Square Players, stated, "We have only one policy in regard to the plays we produce—they must have artistic merit. Preference will be given to American plays. . . . Though not organized for purposes of profit, we are not endowed. Money alone has never produced an artistic theatre. . . . Believing in democracy in the theatre, we have fixed the charge of admission at 50 cents" (Eaton 21). These lines, which were more or less adopted by the Guild in its later form, show a belief in a theatre for the people. What is important to note, however, is the form their idea of the communal will—identified elsewhere as Americanism —takes; it is inextricably bound up with a particular vision of the democratic.

The Guild's early historian/champion/apologist Walter Prichard Eaton suggests, in fact, that the appeal to democracy was a hollow gesture: the founders of the Washington Square Players didn't expect anyone would be willing to pay more than fifty cents. However, he goes on to add that the "democratic" experiment was more genuine in the sense that "[i]t rose spontaneously from the desires of the actual workers for a chance at self-expression, and looked for audience to men and women like-minded in discontent with the existing playhouse. Probably the desire for self expression, too, was a bit stronger than the discontent with existing conditions" (22). The Guild, following the policies of the earlier group, was not by inclination a political theatre. Rather, the Guild's production of political plays (the number of which increased after the stock-market crash of 1929) is very much in keeping with a moderate progressivist belief in democracy, guided by intellectuals using philosophy as an instrument of social betterment, controlled by middle-class values, and to a certain extent, exclusionist. In short, it was structured much like the dominant conception of political democracy current in the 1920s, with its distrust of radical leftism and its striving for a truly American culture based on European models.

The Guild, with a stated preference for European plays, believed that there was something inherently progressive about doing the newest and best drama, regardless of social message or country of origin. As Joseph Wood Krutch put it, they were "more conspicuously bohemian than revolutionary" (228). To be sure, in addition to the numerous important productions of nonpolitical European plays, the Guild did produce politically oriented dramas from both sides of the Atlantic, including Elmer Rice's *The Adding Machine* and world premieres of Shaw's *Heartbreak House* and *St. Joan*. But the Guild's primary focus was the creation of high-quality drama that would elevate as much as express the tastes of its audience, that would expose them to a great tradition of European drama that might, in time, call forth an American equivalent. However, given their increasing reliance on a subscription audience, the Guild became more and more enmeshed in the complex negotiations between trying to maintain a consciously artistic progressive theatre and to reflect the tastes and desires of a large audience whose participation was both expressed and mediated by their season subscriptions. Indeed, the decision to move early successful Guild productions to Broadway engendered acrimonious debate among the founders. The question was twofold: how a theatre could produce high-quality drama if it was forced to operate on Broadway principles, and how it could afford to survive if it didn't. As Eaton remarks, "Commercialism, in a sense, it certainly was. But commercialism sometimes means paying your bills" (39). On Broadway, then, the political stands in an ambivalent relationship to both art and commerce. To reach the people, one has to have access to capital; to move them, one has to be able to express their will—although as Wagner noted in his idea of luxury, the will of the Volk is often obscured by the operations of capital.

The Guild's particular brand of political theatre, a sort of bohemian aestheticism, was thus tied through the mechanisms of Broadway to larger conceptions of democracy and the "people." Granted, these conceptions are not radical by the standards of the 1920s (or today, for that matter), but they are part of an attempt in post–World War I America to establish truly American forms in the arts, including music and the visual arts. Levine—who scarcely mentions the Guild in his book—has chronicled the development of the left-wing theories out of the search for a native tradition of drama in the 1910s with the work of Van Wyck Brooks and Waldo Frank, a tradition very much in keeping with the Guild's sense of the artist as guardian of the culture.

In Brooks the study of literature is tied to an understanding of the national consciousness. His advocacy of a literary nationalism is extended in Frank's belief that the theatre is the best form available to present social problems and that Americans should put the theatre to its best use. Political theatre thus acceded to a central position in the progressive conception of literary nationalism, although both Brooks and Frank raised the question of what needs to happen to create a truly representative American theatre. For example, Frank disapproved of the Washington Square Players' dependence on non-American authors, contending that European spirits of revolt were not the same as American spirits of revolt (Levine 14–15). To have truly social merit, American drama needed to develop along its own political lines. Frank's ideal was the ideal of a democratic nationalist drama, progressive in both form and content. His criticism therefore foreshadowed the shift to more overtly political theatre following the Crash. The concept of democracy as contested ground where the need of the "common man" (to borrow a phrase from a Roosevelt campaign speech) requires satisfaction links the idea of literary nationalism to the more political drama of social realism that follows the Crash.

Waldo Frank serves also as a connecting point between the Guild and another Broadway producer of political theatre during the period. The Group Theatre was founded in 1930 by three disenchanted Guild employees: Lee Strasberg, Harold Clurman, and Cheryl Crawford. They took the name from Frank's condemnation of the loss of the communal spirit in modern society. Indeed, the Group was founded in direct opposition to the Guild's elitism; to the Group the Guild was a successful producing organization, but it had lost contact with its audience. It comprised, Clurman argued, "admirers rather than makers, . . . imitators rather than initiators, buyers and distributors rather than first settlers or pioneers" (23). In Clurman's conception a theatre must be able "to translate a philosophy of life into a philosophy of theatre" (32); it must be able to reflect and change the world around it. It must be both communal and political.

The Group was founded, moreover, on a significantly different concept of democracy than was the Guild, as suggested by the names. The Guild, with its conscious associations of a small collective of talented craftspeople producing a useful object for others, is in striking contrast to the Group, which suggests a conscious effort at unity rather than separation. The Group was founded as a theatre collective that would work together over a number of years, developing a mode of work and a body of productions that would build connections with an ever-growing public. Clurman noted that the theatre had as its primary goal the establishment of a community with its audience, whose lives and sympathetic understanding rather than some "abstract standard of artistic or literary excellence" are "the only basis for judgment" (30–31). The Group was a resolutely American theatre, devoted to the development of native forms. Thus, all the plays produced by the Group in its history, save one—Piscator's adaptation of Dreiser's *An American Tragedy*—were written by Americans.

It is not difficult to see how the Group's particular vision comes out of a desire for communal expression coupled with the desire for political action. But the oft-quoted comment made by Mordecai Gorelik that all of the Group's productions centered on the question "What shall it profit a man if he gain the whole world and lose his own soul?" underscores the paradoxical nature of the Group's goals. Whereas Gorelik and the actors pushed for the Group to take more overtly leftist political stands, Clurman and the other directors believed the best way to develop a theatre of the people was to take advantage of the existing apparatus of capitalist theatre and use it for more democratic ends. In her history of the Group Wendy Smith notes that the Group believed "for all its faults, Broadway was the heart of the American theatre, and they wanted to be a part of it. . . . [T]hey wanted to change the mainstream, not abandon it" (Smith 72). These internal tensions, which eventually tore the Group apart, are one result of the inherent problems in attempting to express the consolidated will of a heterogeneous folk, that is, the inherent problems of democracy.

Surely the Group was successful in representing new voices on the stage. Alfred Kazin remarked about one Group production: "Sitting in the Belasco, watching my mother and father and uncles and aunts occupying the stage in *Awake and Sing* with as much right as if they were Hamlet and Lear, I understood at last. It was all one, as I had always known" (Brenman-Gibson 324). Testimony such as Kazin's, however, is undercut by the belief of some Group members that Broadway remained elitist and forbidding: it never became the democratic theatre of the folk they were searching for. As Odets complained to the communist *Daily Worker* in 1937, "I don't think the left theatre belongs on

Broadway. . . . [I]t belongs all over the country in the Federal Theatre, in union halls, in the hinterland. What's the sense in writing plays for a few bourgeois intellectuals on Broadway at $3.30 a head?" (Brenman-Gibson 482).

Odets's pointing to the Federal Theatre Project as the model of a folk theatre highlights the democratic impulse that drove many theatres of the thirties and the ambivalence about how to achieve it. A people's theatre might not work as a Broadway institution, but the radical proletarian theatres were incapable of becoming a democratic theatre because they couldn't reach a large audience (partly for reasons of capital and partly for reasons of content). A year after he blasted Broadway commercialism, Odets conceded that "any excessive partisanship in a play defeats the very purpose of the play itself. To be socially useful in the theatre . . . one cannot be more left than, for instance, La Guardia. . . . [A]n attempt to reach as broad an audience as possible should always be taken into consideration" (Brenman-Gibson 600–601).

Odets's comments offer us a way to consider the development of political theatre within the structures of—indeed, taking as a model—a capitalist democracy. Inevitably, as in Reinelt's conception of communal drama in general, tension exists between message and form. Political theatre on Broadway, especially during the interwar period, is an attempt to negotiate a balance between social causes and artistic expression. Naturally, there were attempts to develop alternative theatres that will express the communal impulse. Probably the most important attempt to develop this kind of theatre outside the structure of Broadway between the wars was the Federal Theatre Project. Innovative projects such as the Living Newspapers, the simultaneous production in seventeen cities of Sinclair Lewis's *It Can't Happen Here,* and the creation of numerous divisions that produced an astonishing variety of high-quality theatre made the Federal Theatre Project in its short life span a successful democratic theatre.

Despite the closing of these theatres, and despite what seems to be a general and perhaps irremediable shift of Broadway theatre away from the political, the Guild and the Group, along with others in the democratic tradition, have left traces that influence the way we continue to think about the place of theatre within a capitalist democracy. The continuing wars about NEA funding, for example, are part of the legacy of the ongoing struggle to establish a democratic art in America. In fact, American theatre history chronicles repeated attempts to find the proper form to express different, constantly redefined conceptions of democracy. The question of how a theatre can be socially progressive and popular, how it can reach a large, heterogeneous audience without losing its critical/political edge, remains under negotiation and will, because the very process of its negotiation is what gives the political theatre life.

Works Cited

Brenman-Gibson, Margaret. *Clifford Odets, American Playwright: The Years from 1906–1940.* New York: Atheneum, 1981.

Clurman, Harold. *The Fervent Years: The Story of the Group Theatre and the Thirties.* New York: Hill and Wang, 1945.

Dukore, Bernard F. *Dramatic Theory and Criticism: Greeks to Grotowski.* New York: Holt, 1974.

Eaton, Walter Prichard. *The Theatre Guild: The First Ten Years.* New York: Brentanos, 1929.

Gassner, John. "Politics and Theatre." Foreword to *Drama Was a Weapon: The Left-Wing Theatre in New York, 1929–1941,* by Morgan Himelstein. New Brunswick, N.J.: Rutgers University Press, 1963.

Himelstein, Morgan. *Drama Was a Weapon: The Left-Wing Theatre in New York, 1929–1941.* New Brunswick, N.J.: Rutgers University Press, 1963.

Krutch, Joseph Wood. *American Drama Since 1918.* New York: Random House, 1938.

Levine, Ira A. *Left-Wing Dramatic Theory in the American Theatre.* Ann Arbor: UMI Research Press, 1985.

McDermott, Douglas. "The Theatre and Its Audience: Changing Modes of Social Organization in the American Theatre." In *The American Stage: Social and Economic Issues from the Colonial Period to the Present,* ed. Ron Engle and Tice L. Miller, pp. 6–17. Cambridge: Cambridge University Press, 1993.

Reinelt, Janet. "Notes for a Radical Democratic Theater: Productive Crises and the Challenge of Indeterminacy." In *Staging Resistance: Essays on Political Theater,* ed. Jeanne Colleran and Jenny S. Spencer, pp. 283–300. Ann Arbor: University of Michigan Press, 1999.

Odets, Clifford. *Six Plays.* New York: Methuen, 1982.

Rabkin, Gerald. *Drama and Commitment.* Bloomington: Indiana University Press, 1964.

Smith, Wendy. *Real Life Drama: The Group Theatre and America, 1931–1940.* New York: Grove, 1990.

A Relationship in Flux

Variety Theatre and Government in the Twentieth Century

Susan Kattwinkel

> I represent the existing instrumentalities of economic influences, whose centrifugal force is implacably hostile to malefactors of great wealth, the fecundity of whose vulpine cunning is, to put it mildly, a confiscatory atrocity whose virulent animosity represents the efforts of oligarchical arrogance, and the turbulent plutocracy of predatory interests to plunge us into a malignant vortex of a species of despotism opposed to economic prosperity, continuity and stability.
>
> —Aaron Hoffman, *My Policies*

VARIETY THEATRE has long been excoriated for its failure to make much deep social or political comment. It has been called "light" theatre and has been scorned for its place as pure entertainment. What are not often discussed are the reasons for this lack of deep social insight and the forms of commentary that did exist. The fact is, throughout the twentieth century variety theatre was the one theatrical form that played successfully to the full range of American tastes and values. As the one place where people of all ethnicities and classes meet, naturally variety theatre must walk a careful line between political awareness and what would be suicidal favoritism.

Variety theatre began the century in a straitjacket, hampered by the same wide appeal that made it successful. Often unable to make direct political commentary, vaudeville performers instead made oblique references to issues of importance to them. And then as the twentieth century progressed and variety theatre went into mass media, and then came out again without the mantle of big business to weigh it down, performers still found themselves hamstrung by the very diversity that made them popular. Instead, variety theatre has chosen to comment on general political tendencies and personalities and to employ metaphor, relying on audiences' desire to see commentary.

In this article I will examine the political commentary found in American variety theatre at the beginning and the end of the twentieth century, tracing the relationship between types of commentary and the pressures experienced by performers at the time. Although the two periods enjoyed similar audiences in terms of economic class, the differences in the geographical diversity of those audiences and in the style of ownership have prompted a significant change in the nature of the political commentary.

Twentieth-century vaudeville looked very different from nineteenth-century vaudeville. In the nineteenth century small, local audiences allowed vaudeville performers, many of whom traveled but rarely, spending most weeks at their home theatre, to comment on political issues important to the neighborhood audiences. Into the 1890s many vaudeville houses, in New York and elsewhere, presented elaborate afterpieces performed by their own stock companies and/or by visiting performers. These afterpieces, written with the local audiences in mind, deliberately reflected the political and social beliefs of their patrons, making fun of local politicians and laws, noting local scandals, and heroizing the local ethnic majority. And although they had begun attracting middle- and upper-class audiences in the 1880s, the vaudeville audience at the end of the nineteenth century was still primarily working class.

But by the beginning of the twentieth century variety had become big business, managed by businessmen like Edward Albee, who booked performers to travel his entire circuit, which ran throughout the country. Vaudeville had grown up in many ways, and it enjoyed audiences of all classes, ethnicities, and political allegiances. As early as 1901 the *Independent* was writing, "Vaudeville manners are now on a par with those of the parlor. . . . The vaudeville theatres of the Greater New York and of the leading cities of the land are more healthful places of amusement than those which produce problem plays, French comedies, and sex dramas" (qtd. in Zellers 99).

Because twentieth-century vaudevillians traveled more often, naturally their material had to be more national in nature, unless they wanted to adjust their jokes for each individual town. As Douglas Gilbert points out: "Communication of styles, popular songs, and events, political or cultural, was not facilitated by radio, newsreels, or motion pictures. The topical gag of a comic that knocked them in the aisles on Broadway was often incomprehensible in Wichita and points west or south" (135). Not all performers applauded the encroaching heterogeneity. In 1910 *The Player*, the magazine of the vaudeville performers' organization The White Rats, complained that all new performers had to do was "learn a song, learn a few dancing steps, and *borrow* several jokes with another newcomer" (qtd. in Kibler 207).

And unlike the audiences of the nineteenth century, big vaudeville spectators rarely enjoyed allegiances to any particular theatre but visited each according to who was playing any given week. These conditions made direct political commentary difficult because audiences were no longer typified but represented a cross-section of the American public. The performers also ran the risk of offending the wrong people. According to Bernard Sobel, the audience at the Palace, the pinnacle of vaudeville entertainment, was largely by subscription: "Reserved parquet seats downstairs were in demand and the illustrious audience usually included agents, critics and Broadway producers" (qtd. in Sobel 90). For these audiences references to politics, although they played to a sense of moral superiority, had to be generic so as not to put spectators in the awkward position of laughing at their benefactors. It was for these audiences that parodies like the one that begins this article were written. Another example is from *The Irish-American Ex-Congressman,* written in 1911 by Robert L. Landrum, which ends with ex-Congressman Dunderhead saying, "I tell you this world is crammed with wizzards [*sic*] and Politations [*sic*]"; the next stage direction reads, "The Devil appears Stage Center" (Landrum).

Twentieth-century vaudeville walked the line between high-class refinement and low-class sensationalism. Although it tried to woo upper-class patrons without alienating its working-class roots, it problematized the hitherto accepted class separations in American society. M. Alison Kibler has written about how this new mix of class appeal challenged gender and cultural hierarchies, and Harley Erdman has written about how it affected the expression of ethnic bias, but it affected the expression of political preference as well.

The desire to keep these higher paying audience members led to strict censoring on the part of theatre managers and owners, who, because of the monopolies they held, could set the standards for content. Manager E. F. Albee was especially particular about content. Earlier managers Tony Pastor and B. F. Keith had already cleaned up the language and sexual content of their shows, but Albee paid particular attention to political matters. Whereas the afterpieces of the late 1800s had regularly skewered politicians and policies unpopular with the management, Albee made sure that no such commentary jeopardized his standing with the local elite. He once canceled "a play concerning fraudulent divorce laws" (Sobel 67). When the YMCA was involved in a scandal following World War I, Albee prevented any of his artists from making fun of the organization, calling such criticism "un-American" (Gilbert 386).

In his survey of vaudeville, performer Joe Laurie lists lines cut from vaudeville acts during the second cleanup of vaudeville in the late 1920s. Included are "[a]ll references to Mayor Walker and LaGuardia, although used innocently enough. Unfavorable comments have been received by our patrons" and "Name of President Hoover or any state, city, or national official" (Laurie 288, 292). Max Beerbohm's list of things that make an audience laugh in vaudeville, written in *Living Age* in 1902, does not include anything remotely connected to politics, although it did include ethnic and gender-oriented jokes.

The direct political references that did exist appeared mostly in the acts of the monologuists like Lew Dockstader and Cliff Gordon, whose sometimes blue humor and dangerous commentary were tolerated because of the performers' popularity. The monologue *My Policies*, quoted at the beginning of this article, features humor such as the metaphor, if such a term can be so loosely used, of the Politician Bird, who "as a rule flies in a very crooked line. . . . They don't like the sunlight. But you'll always find them congregated where things are shady . . . by jingling a few coins together, you can generally coax them to play with you" (Hoffman). But in material added to the original text by performer Lew Dockstader in 1914, there are several cutting jokes at the expense of specific New York politicians who were running for election. Labeled "New York State Election Locals," the material indicates that at least some specific political commentary was still being supplied for local audiences. Had Dockstader gone on tour at that time, however, much of this particular monologue would have been useless, and another manager might have forbidden it.

When variety entertainment reemerged from the television set into wide popularity in the 1980s, it was no longer hampered by business owners with personal interests to protect. The artists were running their own shows and were free to adopt any relationship to the government they desired. But what they still had in common with the twentieth-century vaudeville performer was a diverse audience, covering every possible sector of the American class structure. They attracted middle- and lower-class audiences from the growing world of stand-up comedy, and upper-class audiences through the relationship they maintained with traditional theatrical structures.

But although this diversity insured them audiences then rarely seen in traditional theatres, it also made direct political commentary difficult, especially given the largely conservative nature of the country at that time. This audience also moved. More often than not spectators at late-twentieth-century variety theatres were tourists, taking in some theatrical entertainment between gambling and relatives. It was dangerous to rely too heavily on the parody of local politicians when much of the audience might be from out of town. But one thing the American public has always had in common, in spite of differences in political or social beliefs or sophistication, is a suspicion of government and politicians in general. So although biased political commentary was often counterproductive, these artists could ridicule figures of national importance (as long as any one group did not receive the majority of the attention) and use the metaphors of popular theatre to encourage spectators to question their assumptions about political structures.

Two of these contemporary variety artists are the magicians Penn and Teller, who first achieved nationwide visibility in the early 1980s and who are still widely popular. Known as "the Bad Boys of Magic," they create a metaphor of magic as deception that they can apply to any social system they want to question. Whereas most magicians insist on maintaining the fiction of "magic" and of possessing special skills (what Penn Jillette calls "arcane knowledge"), Penn and Teller present themselves as just a "couple of very eccentric guys who have learned how to do real cool things" (Dykk 2; Winer 66). They are especially adept at manipulating the levels of fiction perceived by their spectators and at using that manipulation to challenge audiences to join them in a community of skeptics.

At several points in their performances they show their audience how they do those real cool things and continually remind us that sleight of hand or mouth is not only possible onstage. They make constant analogies to contemporary political and new-age con artists. They are not, however, magicians who simply do tricks and then reveal their methods, comparing the tricks to real-life scams. The fiction in a Penn and Teller performance is layered; new fictions emerge even as the magicians expose truths. Apparent revelations turn out to contain further mysteries, and one is always left wondering at what point the two men have told the truth. The simultaneous demystification and deception supplies the raw materials, and the performers rely on the intelligence of their audiences to carry their growing skepticism out of the theatre and into their responses to authority figures.

This respect for the audience lies behind everything Penn and Teller do in their shows. They call themselves confidence men and con artists, and while they're admitting it they're also showing the audience how to do it too, as well as warning them to watch out for con men everywhere. Their allusions to everyday life and their analogies of themselves to the hucksters of politics encourage the audience to be skeptical of anyone trying to sell them something. When Penn and Teller perform the traditional cup-and-ball trick with clear cups, describing their palming technique throughout, and the scam is still not visible, the process illustrates the sleight of hand and verbal distraction one can achieve with a little practice. Ron Jenkins, in his book *Acrobats of the Soul,* sums up the effect: "While the audience members may not be transformed from suckers to skeptics overnight, they might be a little more prone to laugh the next time a politician or salesman tells them there's nothing up his sleeve" (176).

The political nature of the demystification becomes clearer when the decisions made by volunteers for particular tricks are revealed as coming not from their free will but from their unwitting manipulation. Penn often talks, in performance, about the concept of "force" used often by magicians, although never overtly, to insure that the correct card is picked by the audience member, who assumes that he or she is asserting free will. Penn and Teller connect this idea to advertising and politics, where consumers are "forced" to believe that their own free choice of a product or person will lead to a better life. In an example supplied by Ron Jenkins, Penn asks a man to pick a card, and then when he "insists that he has made a free choice, Penn mocks his innocence. 'You must have loved the last election,' he barks" (Jenkins 176).

Jillette's negotiation of the lines between fictions is precarious, as he lies even while admitting he is lying, inducing suspicion of all that he says. In the patter that accompanies Jillette's fire-and-broken-bottle juggling he explains why juggling fire is so easy (the wands are weighted correctly) and why juggling broken bottles is so hard (they are weighted variously and poorly for juggling). At each performance he pays special attention to one bottle, saying that it really is hard to juggle and that he says that every night but that at this performance he really means it; but of course he says that at every show too, so it is nearly impossible to make the audience believe him. He even pretends to show someone offstage how difficult it is. Online testimonials of spectators indicate Penn's talent at this patter, for very often spectators believe him, feeling that normally this patter is just a hoax but that in this particular case he was telling the truth. Of course those same testimonials also reveal that to some extent at least, the point isn't getting through.

The implicit message throughout their performances is one of, in Teller's words, "using your head in a world full of flim-flam" (Trillin 80). Both men are fascinated by the concept and methods of lying and with the many ways of exposing lies. Most important to them in performance is to not lie to their audience, or to tell them up front when they are lying, and then to deceive them nevertheless. They cultivate the dual nature of their performances, where they admit to the lies, even as they perform them, simultaneously enlightening and duping their spectators. The entertainment and the education come in the successful performance of a trick even while it is being explained.

Further complicating the assumptions made in traditional magic acts are Penn and Teller's appearance. The two wear gray suits with red "power ties," giving the appearance of lawyers or stockbrokers out for a drink after work. Undermining this impression are Jillette's ponytail (although that too was popular in the corporate world in the mid-1980s) and his one red fingernail. Costume designer Holly Cole has called the look "hyper-conservative" and considers it part of their desire to "ridicul[e] the hype, yet dazzl[e] and mystify you at the same time" (Cole 6).

Although Penn and Teller's deconstruction of American assumptions is decidedly more sophisticated than the direct attack of nineteenth-century vaudeville, there were groups in the late twentieth century whose political commentary had the familiar look of parody. One of these groups is Esther's Follies of Austin, Texas. Popular with local and tourist audiences since the late 1970s, the group makes fun of any political figure in the news, making sure to give equal time to all political parties so as not to alienate spectators.

The performance of Esther's Follies is very much in the style of late-nineteenth-century vaudeville, with the majority of the performers on any given week members of the home company. The company perceives its audience as very diverse—both Austinites and tourists—and "more of a combination of comedy club and watching comedy on television, than a theatre-going, audience" (Sedwick). The writers are very careful to make all their political commentary equal-opportunity, ridiculing Democrats as often as Republicans, and generally focusing on contemporary events and scandals rather than on any ongoing issue of importance to company members.

At times the company has written true burlesques,[1] using songs (with

---

[1]The term *burlesque*, although generally evoking the scantily clad striptease spectacles of the late 1860s through the 1910s, is also used in the language of vaudeville to describe parodies of well-known plays that were performed using some original music and dialogue but that parodied the style and content of the original play. Because of the laxness of copyright laws, it was easy for vaudeville managers to acquire scripts of the latest sensations or to hire someone to go to the theatres and transcribe the plays. New words would be put to the music and the result called a burlesque. The relationship between this type of burlesque and the "girly show" is well articulated in the Fields's *From the Bowery to Broadway*.

revised lyrics) and content and style references from a familiar musical or film to poke fun at news-making figures, fads, or political issues. Perhaps the best example of this was their production of "The Rocky Clinton Horror Show," a fifteen-minute musical that they used as their first-act closing number for several months in 1993 and 1994 and revived for the 1996 presidential campaign, both pre- and postelection. This number focused on President Clinton and his family and the president's attempt to change the way the government was run and the way the country thought, a concept that was in discussion and the national consciousness continuously during the first two years of the Clinton presidency. The original movie is about an alien from the planet Transylvania who comes to Earth to create a new being and who thoroughly shocks everyone who runs into him. Therefore it serves as a good basis for a metaphor of the depiction of Clinton as an alien to Washington society who comes to create new government and shocks everyone in the meantime.

The sketch used the music of the movie, as well as costumes and makeup that parodied it. Each cast member recreated a character from the movie in the image of one of the Clinton or Gore families. Perhaps the most popular moment of the sketch aped the moment in the movie where the lead, Dr. Frank N. Furter, descends in an open elevator in fishnet stockings, high heels, and a bustier. As he descends, he is revealed little by little, first legs, then body, then head, to music that, combined with the reaction from the other characters, reveals him as the movie's central figure. In the Esther's Follies sketch an elevator was also available, normally used for a magic number, and the actor playing Clinton was revealed little by little, wearing high heels, fishnet stockings, American flag briefs, and a coat and tie. The same music from the movie was used, and the other characters onstage performed similar reactions to those in the movie.

Other characters in the parody also represented well-known political figures. George Bush provided a counterpoint to Clinton. And the company was careful in its portrayal of Texas governor Ann Richards, who was as hated as she was revered. Although the song about her portrayed her as strong and intelligent, the character appeared onstage in pasties and tassels. The original movie itself was also chosen because of its supply of a metaphor that the writers could not resist. In the movie Dr. Frank N. Furter creates a monster named Rocky. In the burlesque of the piece one of the highlights was when the "creature" created by Clinton turned out to be Ross Perot.

Metaphor and the parody of national political figures are common throughout contemporary variety theatre. Hampered, like early-twentieth-century vaudeville, by the diversity of the very audience that makes it possible, its performers cannot risk much direct, biased political commentary. Instead, they ridicule the system of government and the national figures that represent it in order to encourage questioning on the part of their spectators. If they succeed, then audiences begin to approach the government and politicians with the enthusiasm of Aaron Hoffman's 1914 Senator Boob, who encourages "every citizen [to] feel extinction when he looks up and knows he is under the protection of the glorious stars and tripe" (Hoffman).

Works Cited

Beerbohm, Max. "The Laughter of the Public." *The Living Age,* 5 April 1902, pp. 52–57.

Cole, Holly. "Costume Design and the New Vaudevillians." *Theatre Design & Technology* 22.2 (1986): 6.

Dykk, Lloyd. "Penn and Teller." *Vancouver Sun,* 22 July 1993, p. 2C1.

Erdman, Harley. *Staging the Jew: The Performance of an American Ethnicity, 1860–1920.* New Brunswick, N.J.: Rutgers University Press, 1997.

Fields, Armond, and L. Marc Fields. *From the Bowery to Broadway: Lew Fields and the Roots of American Popular Theatre.* New York: Oxford University Press, 1993.

Gilbert, Douglas. *American Vaudeville: Its Life and Times.* New York: Dover, 1940.

Hoffman, Aaron. *My Policies.* [1915.] 29 July 2000 <http://memory.loc.gov/ammem/amhome.html>.

———. *Speaker of the House.* [1913.] 29 July 2000 <http://memory.loc.gov/ammem/amhome.html>.

Jenkins, Ron. *Acrobats of the Soul.* New York: TCG, 1988.

Kibler, M. Alison. *Rank Ladies: Gender and Cultural Hierarchy in American Vaudeville.* Chapel Hill: University of North Carolina Press, 1999.

Landrum, Robert L. *The Irish Ex-Congressman.* [1911.] 29 July 2000 <http://memory.loc.gov/ammem/amhome.html>.

Laurie, Joe. *Vaudeville: From the Honky-Tonks to the Palace.* New York: Holt, 1953.

Sedwick, Shannon. Interview by author. Austin, Tex. 18 April 1995.

Sobel, Bernard. *A Pictorial History of Vaudeville.* New York: Citadel Press, 1961.

Trillin, Calvin. "A Couple of Eccentric Guys." *New Yorker,* 15 May 1989.

Winer, Linda. "Penn and Teller: Up to Their Old Tricks." *Newsday,* 4 April 1991.

Zellers, Parker. *Tony Pastor: Dean of the Vaudeville Stage.* Ypsilanti, Mich.: Eastern University Press, 1971.

Disrupting the Spectacle

French Situationist Political Theory and the Plays of Howard Brenton

John O'Connor

HOWARD BRENTON WAS ONE of a number of "second wave angry young men" who emerged out of London's thriving fringe theatre scene in the 1960s. A committed socialist, his plays provide a critique of a world that, in his words, "is in thrall to a system that respects nothing but money and power" (*Plays: One* xiii–xiv). Brenton's plays expose the contradictions inherent in capitalism and engage in an analysis of possible responses to the system.

Early in his career Brenton alluded to the influence of the French situationists, a Marxist group instrumental in the Paris student riots of May 1968. He said in a 1975 interview, "A lot of ideas in *Magnificence* [Brenton's first major work, commissioned by the Royal Court Theatre] came straight out of the writing at that time in Paris, and the idea of official life being like a screen. . . . The situationists showed how gigantic the fraud is" (Itzin and Trussler 20). It was at this time that his work began to describe and critique British culture from the perspective of French situationist political theory.

Guy DeBord's *Society of the Spectacle*, first published in France in 1967, provides a definition and analysis of this theory. DeBord was a Marxist theorist and critic and edited the journal *Internationale Situationniste* from 1958 to 1969. The theory behind the "society of the spectacle" explains the lack of a working-class revolutionary consciousness in the postwar West. The working class has been bought off by material and ideological bribes created by the capitalist class. The situationists approach revolutionary politics from the point of consumption of bourgeois ideology rather than from the point of production. The theory addresses the problem of the alienation of all classes of people from themselves, and from each other, instead of the problem of the exploitation of the working class. Revolution involves first a consciousness of the spectacle and how it operates, then a denial of its power to control society.

What is the spectacle, exactly? According to DeBord, "In societies where modern conditions of production prevail, all of life presents itself as an immense accumulation of spectacles" (par. 1). Every aspect of public life is a part of this accumulation, from the goods and services people consume to the sporting events they watch or participate in, from the news programs produced on television to the choices people are presented with at the polls. The spectacle is an affirmation of the capitalist system, and its function is to maintain that system. It denies individual freedom and creativity by presenting itself as the only viable way of life available. It "expresses what society *can do,* but in this expression the *permitted* is absolutely opposed to the *possible*" (DeBord par. 25).

Economically, politically, and culturally, the spectacle allows people to make choices that are not real. They believe they have the freedom to choose a career, and this freedom gives them a sense that they can do anything. But in reality the choices they have are limited by innumerable conditions, including the quality of education they can afford, their social background, and the pressures imposed by their parents, peers, and a system that measures success in terms of material wealth.

Their choices are also limited on the political front. Each year the distinctions between political parties and their platforms become less clear. The voter's choice is limited to options that will maintain the status quo. The spectacle allows opposition only to the extent that the system will remain intact. Even when opportunities to effect significant social or political change do arise, the spectacle is able to absorb the changes and so perpetuate itself, as in the New Deal policies of the Roosevelt administration and the socialist economic reforms of the Labour government.

The spectacle controls people's cultural choices, as well as their economic and political choices. The sheer volume of movies, television and radio programming, newspapers and magazines, and sporting and cultural events contributes to a system rooted in consumption. All aspects of culture and entertainment are leveled by the overwhelming necessity to make a profit. Even news programs are subject to "ratings wars," so news becomes sensational entertainment, a commodity to be consumed. The spectacle presents an endless array of choices that maintain an illusion of freedom while suppressing individual creativity.

Even history has been subjugated and put into the service of the spectacle: "History remains separated from the common reality. . . . The masters who *make history their private property,* under the protection of myth, possess ownership of the mode of illusion" (DeBord par. 132). Wars are presented as heroic struggles for freedom waged by tough yet benevolent leaders and their loyal, fearless troops. The reality of the horrors of war, the death and destruction, is romanticized and sentimentalized in movies and popular fiction, or it is characterized on the evening news as sterile technological supremacy. The destruction of Native American culture and society becomes the fulfillment of a nation's destiny. Criminals, murderers, and swindlers are represented as romantic antiheroes, and their lives become sensational entertainment.

All aspects of the spectacle work together to maintain the power of the capitalist system and those who control that system. The subjugation of those who are not in control is achieved by their isolation from one another. The increasing emphasis on job specialization in the capitalist system fosters isolation in the workplace, as does the reliance on expanding networks of electronic communications systems such as fax machines and e-mail. Additionally, society's glorification of rugged individualism and the spirit of competition contributes to a sense of isolation in all aspects of daily life: "The technology is based on isolation, and the technical process isolates in turn. From the automobile to television, all the *goods selected* by the spectacular system are also its weapons for a constant reinforcement of the conditions of isolation" (DeBord par. 28). This isolation accomplishes the desired goal of effectively preventing a unity of opposition to the capitalist system. It creates a society of consumers who compete against each other in an unending struggle to obtain material wealth, to achieve the goals imposed by the system.

Under capitalism economic necessity has been "replaced by the necessity for boundless economic development," and the fulfillment of primary human needs has been "replaced by an uninterrupted fabrication of pseudo-needs" (DeBord par. 51). The result is alienation of individuals from society and from themselves, for the more the spectator "accepts recognizing himself in the dominant images of need, the less he understands his own existence and his own desires" (DeBord par. 30). All members of the society of the spectacle, even those who are in control, are alienated from themselves and from each other. All are in the thrall of a system based on material consumption and the endless accumulation of products, a system that measures success only in terms of wealth and possessions. The spectacle is the reflection of that system; in fact, it is "the impoverishment, servitude and negation of real life . . . the expression of the separation and estrangement between man and man. . . . It is the highest stage of an expansion which has turned need against life" (DeBord par. 215).

The capitalist system and the society of the spectacle created to maintain its power cannot be overcome easily. The system has the ability to absorb change and to eventually turn change to its own advantage. The situationists point to the Russian Revolution as proof that "the bourgeoisie created an autonomous power which, so long as its autonomy lasts, can even do without a bourgeoisie" (DeBord par. 106). The Bolsheviks simply replaced the bourgeois ruling class with a bureaucracy, and private property became the collective property of the bureaucratic class. Isolation and alienation were an integral part of the system, and political corruption and manipulation of individuals were used by the ruling bureaucracy to maintain power and control.

Successful socialist revolution cannot take place without the formation of a revolutionary movement that recognizes that "it *does not represent* the working class. It must recognize itself as no more than a radical separation from the *world of separation*" (DeBord par. 119, DeBord's emphasis). In other words, revolution entails a consciousness of the spectacle and a denial of the power of the spectacle to control individual lives. Violent attempts to seize power and anarchistic actions that see a proletarian revolution as immediately present fail to acknowledge the power of the spectacle. Radical consciousness must precede radical action. And radical action is not anarchic but involves raising the consciousness of all members of society by presenting them with a critical analysis of the spectacle and how it functions: "The revolutionary organization can be nothing less than a unitary critique of society, namely a critique which does not compromise with any form of separate power anywhere in the world, and a critique proclaimed globally against all the aspects of alienated social life. . . . [I]t cannot reproduce within itself the dominant society's conditions of separation and hierarchy. It must struggle constantly against its deformation in the ruling spectacle" (DeBord par. 121).

The goal of a socialist revolution is to restore people to themselves and to each other, to replace authoritarian or acquisitive societies with ones that foster human potential and creativity and encourage cooperation, not competition. Socialism aims to replace individual greed and moral bankruptcy with an emphasis on moral responsibility. Socialist writer E. P. Thompson explains: "Socialism is not only one way of organising production; it is also a way of producing 'human nature.' . . . The aim is not to create a socialist State, towering above man and upon which his socialist nature *depends,* but to create an '*human* society or socialised humanity' where (to adapt the words of More) man, and not money, 'beareth all the stroke'" (29).

Society of the Spectacle provides the theoretical basis for an analysis of Brenton's political philosophy as it is presented in his plays. The short early works expose the fraud of the spectacle and attempt to portray a reflection of the isolation and alienation of capitalist society. Beginning with *Magnificence,* Brenton's analysis becomes more sophisticated. He exposes more elements of the spectacle and probes their mechanics in greater depth. He also presents alternative ways of combating the spectacle and analyzes their effectiveness. The nature of revolution becomes a major theme in these later works. Finally, Brenton completes his critique of the spectacle by presenting alternatives to it in his utopian plays. These works not only expose the fraud of the spectacle and explore the nature of revolution; they present a vision of human nature motivated by moral responsibility and concern for the dignity of women and men.

Brenton's aim is to expose the contradiction between the spectacle and reality, to portray the struggles of men and women who are striving to maintain human dignity and integrity, and to present alternative ways of looking at the world. His ultimate goal is to change the consciousness of his audience. There is a contradiction inherent in this goal, however, because theatre itself constitutes a part of the spectacle. Brenton is thus faced with the task of revealing the fraud of the spectacle within the context of the spectacle itself.

Brenton experimented with this contradiction in his early plays, written for fringe theatre companies. These groups were small, usually touring, companies whose aim was to bring theatre to universities, festivals, and working-class audiences. They were consciously formed to provide a thematic and stylistic alternative both to the mainstream, middle-class commercial theatre of London's West End and the establishment theatre of the major subsidized companies. As an alternative to the spectacle presented by these bourgeois institutions, the fringe groups reached an audience that, in most cases, was sympathetic to the political and social content of their productions. The stylistic experimentation also met with favorable audience responses.

For these groups Brenton wrote small plays that required very little technical support. They are plays for a "poor theatre" that reflect the moral and social decline of post–World War II English society. But these small plays began to burst at the seams, both thematically and stylistically, as Brenton's political consciousness grew. The urge to go beyond the simple description of society to the dialectical exploration of the relationships at the root of society led Brenton to write for larger theatre venues. He explains, "You just can't write a play that describes social action with under ten actors. With fifteen you can describe whole countries, whole classes, centuries" (Itzin 187).

Brenton's decision to write for larger theatres was also motivated by the fact that the fringe was beginning to be assimilated. Pip Simmons, a noted fringe director, said in 1975, "The English are very good at absorbing everything. I mean, they've absorbed us" (Ansorge 76). The spectacle was co-opting the fringe, making it fashionable and artistically avant-garde, and overlooking its politics. Brenton said in a 1973 interview that the fringe began to fail when audiences "became theatrically literate and the discussions afterwards stopped being about the plays' content and began to be about their style" (Hammond 27).

Brenton began to see that to challenge the spectacle he needed to attack it at its source, to reveal the fraud of the spectacle within the spectacle itself. And he also came to realize that the goal of consciousness-raising cannot be accomplished by speaking to a small, sympathetic audience. The fringe audiences were already politically aware for the most part. The reactionary establishment audience of the mainstream English theatre was not. The opportunity to write for the major subsidized theatres provided Brenton with an essential tool he believed he needed to portray social action, a large stage, and it gave him the chance to speak to a huge audience. Brenton wanted to write for the large, subsidized theatres because "theatre belongs to the centre of public life—and should be as loud as parliament. That is what a big theatre should be . . . big in order for large numbers of people to see it and for it to begin to reverberate, for it to be discussed, for it to be a national event, for it to be news" (Itzin 192). In other words, large theatres should be as loud and powerful as the spectacle itself.

Jed, a character in *Magnificence,* relates the story of a drunk in a movie theatre who becomes upset at the film and throws a bottle through the screen. Jed uses this story to illustrate a political point he is making about the need for revolutionary action that will "disrupt the spectacle" (Brenton, *Magnificence* 62). Brenton's plays represent his attempt to do that, to break through the spectacle to get at the truth it conceals. But the spectacle exerts an incredible, almost unbreakable influence on life, and truth can often jar the senses with its ugliness and violence.

Brenton disrupts the spectacle and his audience's complacency toward it in a number of ways. Thematically, he explores how the spectacle works in life: *The Churchill Play* and *The Romans in Britain* show how education and history are manipulated by political leaders and others who hold the reins of power; *Magnificence* and *Weapons of Happiness* show how the spectacle absorbs and co-opts opposing viewpoints and how the glorification of competition affects human relationships. In these plays Brenton illustrates the pervasive, almost independent, nature of the spectacle by portraying all people as victims, even those who are seemingly in power. In his later utopian plays, *Sore Throats, Bloody Poetry*, and *Greenland*, his characters discover ways to expose and overcome the spectacle's control of their lives.

Brenton breaks through the spectacle stylistically by reversing his audience's expectations. For example, *Magnificence*, written specifically for the Royal Court, begins as a naturalistic drama. The Court had been a major producer of the works of Arnold Wesker and others who wrote in the naturalist vein. Court audiences had come to expect this kind of work from the theatre and so were able to connect with *Magnificence* quite readily. But the second scene takes place in front of a drop and resembles a music hall comedy routine, and scene four is an empty stage on which two characters glide about in a small boat, chatting. Brenton fulfilled audience expectations by reinforcing the spectacle and then disrupted both the spectacle and expectations. The audiences confronted with this disruption are forced to analyze the reasons behind it and to look critically at the relationships among the scenes.

Brenton's treatment of characters reflects this urge to express life truthfully while disrupting audience expectations. Many critics have condemned him for writing caricatures rather than psychologically complete characters. But Brenton's concern is with how people behave as social beings who act and are acted upon. Theories of human psychology are simply a part of the spectacle because they deny the reality and complexity of socially motivated human behavior. Psychology provides formulas that often easily and reasonably explain human behavior.

Brenton rejects psychology because he feels that human behavior is more complex and ultimately less knowable than psychological theories suggest. He also believes that human action is social action and that sociological and political analyses are more valid than psychological analysis. Additionally, Brenton feels that psychology, as a part of the spectacle, often offers excuses for human behavior and so denies the truth of moral responsibility. His characters disrupt the spectacle of psychological theory, and the realistic theatre that uses that theory, and so disrupt audience expectations: "My characters—my policemen for example—are often more realistic than is thought. The trouble is that the audience's expectations are pallid—they want to admire and respect the characters on the stage and if they are presented with ordinary people as they really are, they often think they are being presented with caricatures" (Kerensky 224).

Brenton's work has also been attacked because it is violent, many critics believing that he espouses violence as a means to achieve socialism. Yet the plays are violent only because they reflect life truthfully. They are not about violence, nor do they condone it; but they do present violence as a symptom of a morally bankrupt society. Brenton tries to show what violence can do to humanity. He does not want his audience to focus on the violence itself but on its causes and its results. He is also making a strong point about the nature of violence in society and how it is portrayed in popular literature, movies, television programs, and even the nightly news. Brenton uses the "publicness" of live theatre to show the immediate reality and effect of violence. When people view violent acts on film or on television, in a dark movie theatre or in the privacy of their homes, it is easy for them to turn violence off, to treat violence as if it were unreal. People have become desensitized to the acts and their effects. Violence has become a part of the mind-numbing spectacle. But it cannot be ignored so easily when it is made real and public.

Brenton's treatment of violence also serves another purpose; it contributes to the dialectical structure of his plays. The socialist artist must represent that which is most base about human nature in order to lead the audience to a better understanding of humanity's potential for goodness. As a socialist writer, Brenton assumes responsibility for presenting the contradictions inherent in the society of the spectacle, and these contradictions cannot be presented as one-sided arguments. People will never fully understand the urgent necessity for change until they fully grasp the depths into which humanity is capable of sinking. Brenton makes the point quite clearly in his preface to *Greenland:* "My instinct was that if you are going to show people moving towards a transformation into citizens of a Utopia . . . you have to show them first at their vilest and their most unhappy. A playwright who shirks from writing about people at their worst, will not be believed when trying to write about them at their best" (3).

This statement can be applied to all of Brenton's work. It reflects his political and artistic growth by speaking both to the inherent dialectical nature of the truthful portrayal of reality and to the necessity for providing an answer, a vision of the fulfilled potential of human nature, freed from the control of the spectacle. Brenton's writing reflects a movement toward the portrayal of a vision of Utopia. The early plays do tend to present people at their vilest and most unhappy, but they can also be viewed from a more positive angle because they represent the beginning of an exploration into the nature of human potential, creative freedom, and moral responsibility.

Works Cited

Ansorge, Peter. *Disrupting the Spectacle*. London: Pitman, 1975.

Brenton, Howard. *Magnificence*. London: Eyre Methuen, 1973.

———. *Plays: One*. London: Methuen, 1986.

———. *Greenland*. London: Methuen Drama, 1988.

DeBord, Guy. *Society of the Spectacle*. Detroit: Black and Red, 1967.

Hammond, Jonathan. "Messages First: An Interview with Howard Brenton." *Gambit* 6.23 (1973): 24–32.

Itzin, Catherine. *Stages in the Revolution*. London: Eyre Methuen, 1980.

Itzin, Catherine, and Simon Trussler. "Petrol Bombs through the Proscenium Arch: An Interview with Howard Brenton." *Theatre Quarterly* 5.17 (spring 1975): 4–20.

Kerensky, Oleg. *The New British Drama*. New York: Taplinger, 1977.

Thompson, E. P. *The Poverty of Theory and Other Essays*. London: Merlin Press, 1978.

A Sort of Nationcoming

Invasion, Exile, and the Politics of
Home in Modern Irish Drama

Mary Trotter

I N HIS STUDY of modern Irish drama Christopher Murray notes that instead of looking at its theatre as a mirror up to nature, the Irish dramatic movement serves a more complicated, deeply political purpose. "In Irish drama," Murray writes, "the mirror does not give back the real; it gives back *images* of a perceived reality. The play as mirror up to *nation*, rather than to nature in Hamlet's sense, results in a dynamic in process; you have to stop it in freeze-frame to distinguish what happened (history) from what might yet happen (politics). The thing is fluid and proleptic. . . . [Irish] drama helps society find its bearings; it both ritualises and interrogates national identity" (9). Throughout the twentieth century Irish playwrights have reflected and rewritten both the political and theatre histories in Ireland in a continuing effort to help us understand the nation's past and present and to shape its future. And one of the critical factors in Irish dramaturgy, just as it is in Irish politics, is the naming and claiming of place.

To describe Irish history for the past three hundred years is to describe a constant land war as a range of ethnic, political and economic communities have claimed rightful ownership to the same physical spaces. These macroeconomic arguments were felt at the microeconomic level, of course, as farmers were evicted for inability to pay rent to absentee landlords, despite crop failures, or as threats and intimidation from other ethnic groups pushed them off their land. At the same time, individuals felt the social violence of compelled emigration. In his essay "Exiles and Emigrants," Kerby Miller suggests that by the middle of the nineteenth century

Ireland's social adjustments to the exigencies of colonialism and world capitalism—adjustments dictated by external pressures and international inequities—mandated massive, sustained emigration. Put bluntly, emigration became the social imperative of post-Famine Ireland: in reality less a choice than a vital necessity both to secure the livelihoods of nearly all who left and most who stayed and to ensure the relative stability of a fundamentally "sick" society which offered its lower classes and most of its young people "equal opportunities" only for aimless poverty at home or menial labour in slum tenements abroad. (29)

Throughout the late nineteenth century the legacy of invasion, eviction, and emigration had only strengthened opposing national identities within Ireland. Many Irish individuals and groups responded to or resisted these events performatively. A community losing one of its citizens to emigration would throw an "American wake," a celebration of that person's (ending) life in Ireland and a tacit acknowledgment of the unlikelihood of his physical return. At the same time Irish in diaspora communities like New York and Boston celebrated their homeland with huge St. Patrick's Day pageants and parades, which both solidified and built on the increasingly idealized notion of "home" among immigrant Irish populations, transforming (if only for a few hours) the center of American cities into their idealized homelands. In the 1870s and 1880s members of the Land League demonstrated against unfair tenant evictions in the West of Ireland by appearing en masse at the site of an eviction and refusing to allow government authorities to force the impoverished tenants from their land. In Dublin and other towns Irish nationalists made a point of speaking Gaelic rather than English in public places, playing Irish games and buying Irish goods as a means of performing their anticolonial convictions.

Such social dramas (that is, performative actions in the world), with their physical invasion and transformation of everyday space and routine and their conscription of audiences, actors, and spaces, make the non-theatrical theatrical and the theatrical dangerous. Aesthetic dramas (that is theatrical performance contained within the frame of a theatre space and theatrical event) in most cases do not call for an immediate response to crisis in the same way that social dramas do. But in Ireland at the beginning of the twentieth century, the very act of putting on a play was often a political event because playwrights self-consciously constructed and critiqued the crisis of identity within their nation for a politically engaged audience. Indeed, aesthetic theatre in Ireland has been in close communication with the social dramas happening just offstage over the past century.

The modern Irish dramatic movement began in the 1890s as a highly visible branch of the Gaelic Revival. Irish plays and performances in those first decades sought to valorize Irish culture as beautiful, different from that of the colonizer England's culture and reflecting a people both entitled to and capable of self-rule.

The Abbey Theatre was the most famous of these Irish political theatres at the beginning of the twentieth century, but it was only one of many theatre groups, and these theatre companies often had close ties to political organizations like the Daughters of Erin, the Gaelic League, the Irish Republican Brotherhood, and the Socialist Irish Citizen Army. In fact, these particular organizations, like many other Irish nationalist groups at the turn of the century, used theatre for recruitment and propaganda. Despite Yeats's claims that the Irish theatre must create good art before propaganda, dramas throughout this period were intimately related to the political activities of their players and audiences. If Richard Schechner's "infinity loop" worked anywhere, it worked here, where nationalist men and women fought for an independent nation on the streets then witnessed or performed an idea of what that nation might be on the stage. And because Irish theatre was (and is) an active and generally acknowledged vehicle for nation building, it developed minutely self-reflexive semiotic and thematic rhetorics. The legacy of theatre as a site for the construction and critique of national identity continues in Irish theatre companies like the Abbey and Gate Theatres in Dublin, the Druid Theatre Company in Galway, and the Field Day Theatre Company based in Derry.

Although a psychoanalytic critic will remind one that "sometimes a pen is just a pen," on the Irish stage a home space, be it a peasant cottage, an Anglo-Irish big house, or a tenement flat, almost inevitably carries a historically established ideological meaning as allegory for homeland. And although the meanings of these spaces shift over time in light of new events within the nation, home spaces continue even today to bear significant ideological weight on the Irish stage.

This phenomenon is especially true in Irish realism, as Una Chaudhuri writes:

> The realistic stage is not merely the context or background or environment of the dramatic action: it is part of the dramatic logic. That is to say that realism actually lives out, though surreptitiously, the kind of magical thinking that makes a place . . . the cause of the drama's events and transformations. The characters of realism, written to be taken more seriously as "real people" than any characters ever before, perform a very specific

version of the real, in which location is not contingent but profoundly determining. (80)

The domestic setting in Irish theatre determines not only the psychological dynamics of the characters, reflecting the state of the family, but represents a particular image of the state of the Irish nation. Often *home* and *homeland* are interchangeable terms in the context of Irish drama, and playwrights have manipulated their settings—and the interactions of those characters to their surroundings—to comment on the state of the nation. This paper describes how setting has been used as an allegory for the state of the nation in Irish drama during three transitional moments in Irish identity: the prerevolutionary period of the Celtic Revival (1900s), the early years of the establishment of the Free State (1920s), and the period of tremendous economic growth and influx of global capital with the joining of the European Economic Community (1990s). I do not intend to claim that the use of the domestic space as a metaphor for nation is universal in Irish drama or that it is used in the same way across decades. In fact, I hope my examples show a few of the ways it has changed over time. Yet the idea of home and the crisis of dislocation have remained vital themes in Irish realism. Outside the context of Ireland's cultural, political, and theatrical histories, an Irish play's concentration of meaning on "place" may seem a naive, sentimental, or conservative approach to representing Irish experience. Actually, however, many Irish playwrights throughout this century have manipulated the Irish domestic setting and the characters' relationships to it in profoundly meaningful—even radical—ways.

In the early years of the Irish dramatic movement the theatre was painfully aware of the Irish stereotypes prevalent on British and American stages and sought to overturn those stereotypes with more positive representations of Irish life. This quest led to an idealization of the Irish peasant and the culture of the Gaeltacht, or Irish-speaking West of Ireland, celebrated in such forms as the translations of Irish ancient texts and contemporary folktales by Lady Gregory and Gaelic League founder Douglas Hyde. Real or imagined threats to idealized representations of the Gaeltacht, or of rural Ireland generally, met with virulent attacks in the nationalist press or even riots, as was the case for J. M. Synge's plays *The Shadow of the Glen* and *The Playboy of the Western World.*

In dozens (maybe hundreds?) of the dramas written during this period, the action takes place in a one-room peasant cottage, a setting intended to evoke the idealized world of the Irish peasant. Logistically, this setting made a lot of sense. It required no scene changes, and one could evoke different landscapes through a small outdoor image through the set window. Thematically the set focused the drama on the family unit. Often the plays merely glorified the peasant way of life. But many plays showed the home in crisis and the family under threat of displacement because of invasion, eviction, and emigration. Usually in such dramas some outside person or force "invades" the domestic space and creates a crisis that leads to the breakup of the family and—it is implied—the desolation of the home. Irish nationalist audiences recognized that the crisis to the family and home reflected a wider crisis within the nation: the still-fresh memory of famine and eviction in the previous century lingered in the minds of both Ireland's rural and urban populations, and a large percentage of the population still emigrated annually.

In 1905 Padraic Colum's antiemigration play *The Land* caught the imagination of the nationalist community, thanks to the playwright's shrewd distillation of the politics of Irish land tenure, nationalism, and dramatic art. "*The Land*," Andrew E. Malone remarked, "is a bitter comedy, all the more bitter because its author . . . deplored the facts upon which it was based. . . . " (qtd. in Sternlicht 27). Although the obvious theme of the drama is conflict between parents and children, Colum contextualizes that theme in the frame of concrete Irish political issues and events. He sets the play in 1885, shortly after the "land wars" of the 1870s that called for "fixity of tenure, free sale and fair rent" for small tenant farmers. The two sixty-year-old fathers in the piece, Murtagh Cosgar and Martin Douras, celebrate the fact that with the passage of the Land Purchase Act they can buy their land and pass it on to their children. The men's drive to own the land, however, has ironic consequences. Murtagh's obsession with improving his farm has driven all but one "vapid" daughter, Sally, and his youngest son, Matt, away. Martin, on the other hand, has spent less time working his land for his sharp-witted daughter, Ellen, and his likeable, verbose, but not very sensible son, Cornelius, because he was a political activist during the land wars, and he even went to jail for his beliefs.

Murtagh's son, Matt, and Martin's daughter, Ellen, are in love, but Murtagh thinks that Ellen's dowry is not big enough for her to marry his son. The children have plans of their own, however. Matt decides to emigrate to America, and Ellen will work as a teacher for a year in Ireland before joining him, leaving the land to their slow-witted siblings.

In any place but Ireland the conclusion to *The Land* is bittersweet yet ultimately happy. The tradition of European realism urges us to praise Ellen and Matt's choice to seek their fortunes in America. In *Staging*

Place Una Chaudhuri deftly outlines the way this situation would play out in a drama of Ibsen or Chekhov:

> The realist discourse of home relies on a long-standing conceptual structure in which two figures are balanced—and constructed—as opposites: the figure of belonging and exile. The home as house (and behind it, the home as homeland) is the site of a claim to affiliation whose incontestability has been established by a thick web of economic, juridical and scientific discourses—which also construct the meaning of exile. It is a usefully ambivalent meaning: on the one hand, exile is branded by the negatives of loss and separation; on the other, it is distinguished by distance, detachment, perspective. For the individual (and exile is a decidedly individualistic figure) the poetics of exile offers a mechanism whereby suffering is exchanged for a certain moral authority, personal rupture for aesthetic rapture. (12)

But in the context of a nationalist play being performed in the Abbey Theatre, Ireland's self-proclaimed "national house," Ellen and Matt's emigration does not bring "moral authority" or "aesthetic rapture," nor, as in W. B. Yeats's *Cathleen ni Houlihan* (1902), does it lead to the renewal of the land. Instead, it leads to a spiritual stillbirth.

Colum leads us to that conclusion at the close of the play. When the young, bright lovers and Ellen's now-defeated father, Martin, watch silently as Cornelius struggles to find the words to urge a group of local emigrants not to leave Ireland. "Stay on the land," he cries, "and you'll be saved body and soul; you'll be saved in the man and in the nation. The nation, men of Ballykillduff, do you ever think of it at all? Do you ever think of the Irish nation that is waiting all this time to be born? (*He becomes more excited; he is seen to be struggling with words*)" (154). The most articulate Irish are silenced by defeat, whereas the foolish Cornelius struggles to find the right words but is ignorant of the necessary complementary action. Although Chaudhuri talks of European naturalism's use of exile in context of a character's personal choice to stay or go, the emigrating Irish youth in *The Land* are actually participating in a common, historically determined social pattern. They are not making radical and independent life choices but expected ones: Ireland's peripheral status in the world economy compelled a large amount of its population to emigrate to economic centers not just for success but for survival.

Colum's staging of this drama, like the text, foregrounds the sense of rootlessness among Ireland's emigrating youth and the inevitability of their departure. Once again the drama is set in a peasant cottage, but only the fathers, Murtagh and Martin, seem to belong there. As the parents and children interact within the home, a group of young persons preparing to emigrate enter the stage space en masse, share with Ellen and Matt their excitement about leaving for America, then exit in the same way. This group enters twice in the course of the play. Although they are friends of Ellen and Matt and members of their community, they have no immediate connection to the stage space or the main characters in the drama. Thus, they can also be read as a kind of invading army, representing the political, economic, and social forces destroying the family, house, and nation.

Realist peasant dramas were the dominant mode of the Irish dramatic movement in the early years of the movement, to Yeats's regret. Playwrights like William Boyle, T. C. Murray, Lennox Robinson, and St. John Ferguson filled the Abbey repertoire with realist dramas set in rural spaces, but other dramatists gained inspiration in urban environments. In 1925 Sean O'Casey's *Juno and the Paycock* took the familiar idyllic peasant cottage and translated it into a space much more a part of the lives of Dubliners: the Dublin tenement flat. O'Casey sets his play during the years of Ireland's civil war. After the signing of the Anglo-Irish agreement, ending Ireland's war of independence, Irish nationalists split over the partition of six counties in Northern Ireland to remain part of the United Kingdom. Within months the internal quarrel became a two-year firefight between "Free Staters," who accepted the treaty, and "Die-hards," who refused it.

O'Casey crams the disparate attitudes and ideas teeming in 1920s Dublin into the crowded tenement house that is the setting of his drama. Juno Boyle, a working-class woman, tries to hold together "Captain Boyle," her alcoholic husband with a parasitic sidekick named Joxer; her daughter, Mary, who is a member of the worker's union and reads Ibsen; and her son, Johnny, an IRA commandant who lost the use of a hip in 1916 and his entire arm in the Anglo-Irish war. The family's problems seem solved when a distant cousin dies and leaves his money to the family. Just as the money seems to transform their domestic situation (Juno no longer grouses at Boyle for his laziness, and Mary's going on strike is no longer a conflict within the family because she no longer has to work), it transforms their domestic space, as they fill the previously sparse space with "*furniture . . . of a vulgar nature*" (36) that they buy on credit. But the money cannot buffer them from the social conditions of the nation at war, and three domestic invasions lead to the downfall of the family and its ultimate dislocation from home.

Invasion one: Jeremy Bentham, the English lawyer who wrote the cousin's will and tells the Boyles of their fortune, begins to court the daughter, Mary. He impregnates her then heads back to England just before Boyle learns that Bentham's clerical negligence while writing the will cost Boyle his inheritance, now sucked up in lawyer's fees. *Invasion two:* In act 2, as the family celebrates its good fortune, Mrs. Tancred appears on her way to her son's funeral. Although her appearance recollects the "poor old woman," Cathleen ni Houlihan, her story, of the loss of her only son in the civil war (thanks to Johnny turning informer), foregrounds the need for Irish unity rather than serves as a call for men to leave their homes and die for Ireland. *Invasion three:* While Johnny is briefly alone in the house, an IRA officer appears and orders him to attend a military meeting. Johnny refuses to go, crying, "I've lost me arm, an' me hip's desthroyed so that I'll never be able to walk right agen! Good God, haven't I done enough for Ireland?" The officer replies, "Boyle, no man can do enough for Ireland!" (60). At the end of the play, as the furniture men are repossessing the Boyles' credit-bought goods, two IRA irregulars enter and drag Johnny away to kill him for treason.

Thus, the drama ends with Johnny dead, Mary and her mother leaving the community in shame because of Mary's pregnancy, and the house stripped of its furnishings. Into this blank space stumble Boyle and his buddy Joxer, punch drunk and decrying that "the whole worl's . . . in a terr . . . ible state o' . . . chassis" (89). The curtain falls with Boyle's proclamation certainly the case in the microcosm and macrocosm of the play—the barren stage representing the Boyles' emptied apartment becomes a clear metaphor for the barrenness of Irish nationality in the throes of civil war.

Although attention to the ideas of dislocation and home are clearly obvious in still-contested Northern Ireland, recent developments in the Republic of Ireland—the country's joining the European Union; the economic miracle of the "Celtic Tiger," which has created a huge boom in the Irish economy; and, for the first time, the Irish having to worry about people moving into their country as well as moving out—have led to new identity crises and new evaluations of the idea of home. Further, the rise of global capitalism has actually weakened local autonomy within the nation and fostered a rise in emigration to the continent among Ireland's enterprising youth. Jim Mac Laughlin notes, "Since entry into Europe, new institutions, by no means all of which are Euro-based, have emerged to classify, to regulate and to literally re-form Irish society and Ireland itself. Since then, also, the urbanization of Irish society, the industrialization of the Irish economy and Europeanisation of Irish agriculture have created entirely new landscapes of social and economic control in Ireland" (199). More than ever, Irish identity is in a state of self-conscious flux, if not "a state of chassis," as the current republic considers its relation to the North, to the European Union, to other postcolonial countries, to its diasporic communities around the globe, to its past, to its future. As Fintan O'Toole has noted, contemporary Irish theatre is addressing this ambiguity:

> Because we no longer have one shared place, one Ireland, we can no longer have a naturalistic theatre of recognition in which a world is signalled to us through objects and we tacitly agree to recognise it as our own. We must instead have a theatre of evocation in which strange worlds, not our own, are in Yeats's phrase "called to the eye of the mind." Our theatre now is about the business of calling up rather than recreating, and this will demand of us new ways of seeing and new categories of criticism. ("Irish Theatre" 174)

Yet still the idea of home haunts these new plays. Some dramas, like Brian Friel's *Wonderful Tennessee* (1993) and Frank McGuinness's *Dolly West's Kitchen* (1999), evoke a kind of longing for a place to claim as home. Some playwrights write about their characters' relationship to specific Irish locations, which they transform into poetic dreamscapes, like Marina Carr's transformation of the midlands in *Portia Coughlaun* (1996) and Tom Mac Intyre's revamping of a Syngean West of Ireland in *Sheep's Milk on the Boil* (1994). Other dramas, like Martin McDonagh's *The Cripple of Inishmaan* (1998) and Niall Williams's *A Little Like Paradise* (1995), explore ironically the clash between the idealized notion of a pastoral Irish West and the economic and social realities of those communities. And still, the domestic space continues to stand in as an allegory for nation.

Paula Meehan's *Mrs. Sweeney* (1997) explores the challenges confronting Dublin's working class despite (or perhaps because of) Ireland's rapid economic growth. Instead of a peasant cottage in an idealized Irish West, Meehan sets her play in a corporation flat, and it reflects the failure of European Union (EU) funding and the rise in the gross national product to affect positively the lives of Dublin's poorest citizens. Meehan's play is personal, as well as political: much of the drama is influenced by her experience living in the Fatima Mansions in the 1980s (Meehan 464). The drama centers on Lil Sweeney, a Dublin tenement dweller who tries to keep herself and her friends sane and surviving despite such personal crises as her daughter, Chrissie, dying of AIDS, her house being repeatedly burglarized and vandalized, and her husband going mad and thinking himself a pigeon. In many ways Lil Sweeney reflects the matriarch in O'Casey's *Juno and the Paycock*, as she proudly tries to create a stable home life for her family and herself despite the disparate forces destroying her home.

The play begins the way one might think it would end, with the invasion and ransacking of the domestic setting. The curtain rises on two thugs ransacking Lil's flat, even breaking the window and taking the curtains, while Bob Dylan's *How Does It Feel?* plays on the radio. Lil spends the rest of the play actually repairing these and subsequent damages to her home, although she can never keep up with the destruction to her house—or herself and her loved ones—caused by the invasion of local burglars, drugs, AIDS, domestic violence, and state authority. Her friend Mariah stays off drugs and fervently volunteers within the housing project in hope of getting a job at the local community center, but when the center hires someone outside the community for the position, it is clear that she will slip back into drug abuse. This disappointment is predicted early in the play by Lil: "I wouldn't put it past [the city officials] to bring in an outsider [for the job]. All that funny money coming into the flats and the only local getting paid is Rose Doyle for cleaning the community centre two mornings a week" (408). Another friend, Frano, is constantly avoiding her abusive husband. For the All Saints celebration Sweeney and Mariah paint her face to hide her bruises. Even the local priest, Father Tom, has trouble keeping up with the damage. He feels honored by the love and courtesy he receives from the community but feels "more like a politician than a shepherd" (444), because he is too overwhelmed by everyday crises to help organize the people or guide them spiritually in any meaningful way.

The trope of home is also found in the madness of Lil's husband, Sweeney. Here Meehan adapts the seventh-century myth of Sweeney, a king who went mad in battle and spent years afterward living as a bird in the trees and composing poems. Lil's husband was once an active socialist and an owner of champion homing pigeons. But the pressures of life in the flat, exacerbated by Chrissie's six-month decline into death and the killing of his homing pigeons by an unknown vandal, drive him to a similar condition to that of his royal seventh-century namesake. However, whereas Sweeney of the ancient poem lived in nature and was celebrated for a genius in his madness, this Sweeney is trapped in an urban tenement flat, speechless, and with only Lil between him and the state mental health system.

Clearly, the flat is not the only thing falling apart in *Mrs. Sweeney.* This black comedy reflects a spectrum of problems confronting Ireland's working class, and the final scene makes clear that all the characters will only grow more damaged in the coming months, or they will not even survive. Yet the images of Lil with her hammer and nails boarding up the latest damage to her home, or the women making beautiful costumes and flags for an All Saints party out of discarded remnants of fabric, are the images that linger. The play thus exposes the desperate social issues that must be addressed in the "new Ireland," but it also celebrates Lil's heroic struggle not only to survive but to create beauty and meaning for herself and others—to create and maintain a physical and spiritual home.

As the rise of the economy in Ireland in the 1990s began to transform the nation's geographical and ideological landscapes, so did it begin to create new opportunities and challenges for Irish culture. On one hand, these rapid changes are creating a postmodern sense of being outside history, as Fintan O'Toole claims: "The great tradition of Irish writing is silent on the subject of suburbs, so you can slip out from under its shadow. No one has ever mythologised this housing estate, this footbridge over the motorway, that video rental shop. It is, for the writer, virgin territory" ("Introduction" x). Yet he goes on to claim that "[w]e need to shape our lives with some sense of significance, some notion of a journey that ties together past, present and future. If history is not given to us, we need to invent it, to create personal histories, to map out private journeys" (x). This task is not that different from the invention of tradition started by Irish nationalists a century ago. Truly, contemporary Irish playwrights are rising to the task, as they continue to hold the mirror up to nation, to engage with what these new political and geographical landscapes mean in terms of personal and national identity, to grapple with the politics of home.

Works Cited

Chaudhuri, Una. *Staging Place: The Geography of Modern Drama*. Ann Arbor: University of Michigan Press, 1996.

Colum, Padraic. *The Land*. In *Three Plays: "The Fiddler's House," "The Land," "Thomas Muskerry."* Dublin: Maunsel, 1917.

Mac Laughlin, Jim. "The Devaluation of 'Nation' as 'Home' and the Depoliticisation of Recent Irish Emigration." In *Location and Dislocation in Contemporary Irish Society: Perspectives on Irish Emigration and Irish Identities in a Global Context*, ed. Jim Mac Laughlin, pp. 179–208. Notre Dame: University of Notre Dame Press, 1997.

Meehan, Paula. *Mrs. Sweeney*. In *Rough Magic: First Plays*, ed. Siobhan Bourke, pp. 397–473. Dublin: New Island Books, 1999.

Miller, Kerby A. *Emigrants and Exiles*. New York: Oxford University Press, 1985.

Murray, Christopher. *Twentieth Century Drama: Mirror Up to Nation*. Manchester: Manchester University Press, 1997.

O'Casey, Sean. *Juno and the Paycock*. In *Collected Plays*. Vol. 1. London: Macmillan, 1963.

O'Toole, Fintan. "Introduction: On the Frontier." In *Dermot Bolger: Plays: 1*. London: Methuen, 2000.

——. "Irish Theatre: The State of the Art." In *Ireland: Towards New Identities?* ed. Karl-Heinz Westarp and Michael Boss, pp. 165–74. Aarhus, Denmark: Aarhus University Press, 1998.

Sternlicht, Sanford. *Padraic Colum*. Boston: Twayne, 1985.

No Curtain. No Scenery

Thornton Wilder's *Our Town* and the Politics of Whiteness

Jeff Turner

I N 1981 THE WOOSTER GROUP premiered *Route 1 and 9 (The Last Act)*, an experimental and highly controversial deconstruction of Thornton Wilder's 1938 play *Our Town*. Conceived and directed by Elizabeth LeCompte, The Wooster Group's complicated pastiche juxtaposed a number of disparate elements: an educational video depicting a college professor providing a traditional humanist analysis of Wilder's play; a reconstruction of a Pigmeat Markham comedy routine (performed by four white actors in blackface); a group of stagehands arranging chairs on the stage for the third act of Wilder's play; a group of blindfolded men attempting to build a house frame; video imagery of a drive through the New England countryside on Routes 1 and 9; video imagery of a pornographic film; and video imagery of scenes from *Our Town*. The porn film and blackface routines were utilized to point up Wilder's "universal" themes and render his portrait of America to expose a culture that is puritanical, uptight, cold, inhibited, and dehumanized. As David Savran has written: "Any interpretation of the work which places Wilder, white culture and Puritan restraint on one side, and Markham, black culture and raw vitality on the other, does so by erecting a sharp line between oppressor and oppressed" (31).

As an undergraduate first encountering a description of postmodern theatre practice in the pages of *The Village Voice*, I found The Wooster Group's irreverent approach to theatre both exciting and inspiring. The production of Jack Heifner's *Vanities* currently taking place at my college suddenly seemed so small. The work of The Wooster Group, Robert Wilson, JoAnne Akalaitis, and Richard Foreman in the late seventies and early eighties seemed to point toward the future of theatre in America. A few years later, after reading and rereading Wilder's play, however, I approached *Route 1 and 9 (The Last Act)* from a more critical perspective. Had The Wooster Group misunderstood *Our Town?* Did Wilder's play celebrate white middle-class American hegemony during the 1930s, or did the play interrogate the very idea of whiteness?

The process of othering whiteness involves marking and decentering the white subject to understand how the anxieties of a dominant cultural group are performed both historically and culturally. The examination of whiteness as a fluid practice, as opposed to a stable object around which all others circle, results in marking whiteness as a racial construct. To challenge the privileged position of whiteness in American culture, scholars cannot raise the gaze of the other or provoke the return of the repressed or oppressed but rather must seek out the inconsistencies at work within representations of white subjectivity. As Homi K. Bhabha writes: "The subversive move is to reveal within the very integuments of 'whiteness' the agonistic elements that make it the unsettled, disturbed form of authority that it is—the incommensurable 'differences' that it must protect itself; the violence it inflicts in the process of becoming a transparent and transcendent force of authority" (21).

The results of such analysis, according to Richard Dyer in *White* (1997), is to undercut the way in "which they/we speak and act in and on the world" (2). For Dyer the critical strategy is to make strange the very discourse of power that was thought to be both fixed and invisible. In this essay I will suggest that Thornton Wilder's *Our Town* does just that. The play reveals white America to be a site of contestation. It is a deeply political play that critiques the American desire during the 1930s to reproduce representations of white, bourgeois materialism unfettered by the complexities of modern progress.

On its surface *Our Town* does appear to be a nostalgic lament for lost values in an economically unstable period of American history, still regretting the losses of one war while preparing to enter another. The play begins at dawn with the birth of a baby in the first year of the twentieth century, and the narrative focuses primarily on the courtship and marriage of two teenagers, George Gibbs and Emily Webb. When Emily dies, nine years into her marriage, she is allowed to revisit her childhood and learns the extent to which humans fail to find true significance in the life process. *Our Town*, however, does not invite its viewer (or reader) to yearn for life as it "was." It does not encourage a return to the glorious days of childhood, nor does it encourage audiences to seek solace in the representation of a simpler past. What it attempts to do is acknowledge the sanctity of living for and in the present moment, undermining the play's nostalgic surfaces to reveal

Wilder's frustration with those staid, middle-class audience members who need nostalgic representations to remind them of their own privileged status.

Jed Harris's biographer, Martin Gottfried, has written that during the opening rehearsal of *Our Town*, the young director told his cast that the "key to this play is dryness. Once it gets sentimental, the play goes out the window." Gottfried also reports that Wilder seconded his director, stating, "The nostalgia has to go" (165). A year later, in an interview with John Franchey of the *New York Times,* Wilder remarked that the play was not meant to be a paean to a golden past but a meditation on the instability of time. "In *Our Town* time was scrambled, liberated" (2). Nevertheless, Wilder's Pulitzer Prize–winning drama was perceived and received as a piece of nostalgic Americana that glorified, in the words of Professor Willard (a character Wilder's Stage Manager calls upon to provide the audience with historical facts surrounding Grover's Corners), "English brachiocephalic blue-eyed stock" (15).[1]

Indeed, following its opening at the Henry Miller Theatre on 4 February 1938, Richard Watts Jr. described the play as a "simple and compassionate chronicle of a small New England community" (6). Writing for the *New York Sunday Mirror,* Robert Coleman hailed the play as capturing "the mind and spirit of this country as have few plays of our time" (34). Brooks Atkinson enjoyed Wilder's "idealized portrait" of spiritual America (1), and *New York Sun* critic Richard Lockridge wrote that *Our Town* "reaches back into the past of America and evokes movingly a way of life which is lost in our present turmoil" (28).

A majority of theatre scholars have agreed with these initial reactions, suggesting the strength of *Our Town*'s dramatic action to be its gentle portrayal of "authentic" American values like family, community, optimism, and the importance of the "smallest events in our daily life" (Wilder xi). Francis Fergusson, for example, has written that Wilder's play "preaches the timeless validity of certain old traditional ideas, and his theatre is almost devoid of conflict, wooing its audience with flattery" (553). Jordan Y. Miller and Winifred L. Frazer argue that *Our Town* accomplishes this by offering its audience a glimpse of "the way it once was, or should have been, and the down-to-earth appeal is undeniable. This is New England that has provided the nation with solid stock, making us what we nostalgically believe we are" (239). Thomas E. Porter's reading goes so far as to suggest Wilder's fictional Grover's

---

[1]Willard's colorful description can be loosely translated as white, Anglo-Saxon Protestants.

Corners becomes the center of the universe: "Living in 'our town' includes a social unity and harmony with nature, the fulfillment of the individual within the community. It inculcates patriotism and moral principles and friendly social interchange" (205).[2] Perhaps for these reasons Wilder's play has entered the canon of America's most favored and most produced dramatic works. As theatre historian Gerald Bordman has written, *Our Town* is an American classic, and "its continued appeal can be attributed in good part to its moving depiction of simpler times and simple values" (531).

Although W. David Sievers critiques *Our Town* as a nostalgic "antidote for anxiety" (258), locating the genesis of the play's meaning in the Great Depression, C. W. E. Bigsby argues that the play deals with universal ideas far removed from "ideological presumptions or the immediate practicalities of 1930s America" (260). I suggest both points of view misunderstand the play's purpose. *Our Town* is neither a soothing work that assuages social tensions nor a work that denies its historical context in favor of larger, more eternal themes. I argue that Wilder's play deconstructs the myth of America as a collective of small egalitarian communities, offering a coherent critique of middle-class, Anglo-Saxon, Protestant hegemony.

The frisson that occurs between what 1930s American audiences wanted to believe about their connection to an idealized past and what *Our Town* actually accomplishes reveals Wilder's play to be a vigorous attack on middle-class decorum and suggests white America itself to be an unstable form of authority. Wilder's use of irony subverts the play's nostalgic representations through the playwright's insistence on challenging the tenants of a nostalgic narrative.[3]

One aspect of Wilder's text that scholar Bert Cardullo has so clearly articulated is how well racial and ethnic boundaries are defined and adhered to within the world of the play. The Stage Manager notes that on the other side of the tracks, far removed from the city center, is Polish Town, the Catholic Church, and some "Canuck" families (6).

---

[2]Porter's description is best reinforced in the play by a highly celebrated scene at the end of the first act when George Gibbs's little sister, Rebecca, marvels at a letter that connects her best friend, Jane Crofut, with the "Mind of God" (Wilder 28–29).

[3]Here I am using Linda Hutcheon's definition of *irony* as a "discursive strategy operating at the level of language (verbal) or form (musical, visual, textual)" (10). For Hutcheon irony undermines the stability of an utterance or an image. It undermines meaning by utilizing the language of the dominating discourse it contests. Also, irony can never be separated from the "social, historical and cultural aspects of its contexts of deployment and attribution" (16).

Later, Belligerent Man, a character planted in the audience, asks Mr. Webb, "Is there no one in town aware of social injustice and industrial inequality?" And Mr. Webb, the editor of the town newspaper, answers: "Well, I dunno. . . . I guess we're all hunting like everybody else for a way the diligent and sensible can rise to the top and the lazy and quarrelsome can sink to the bottom. But it ain't easy to find. Meanwhile, we do all we can to help those that can't help themselves and those that can we leave alone" (17).

Cardullo argues that Webb's response appears to be charitable, but, in fact, this "benevolence" assumes that minority citizens in Grover's Corners are simply unable to help themselves as opposed to the possibility that they have been institutionally denied the opportunity to advance. Webb's remarks also suggest Grover's Corners to be a class-driven, segregated community where the diligent and sensible (explicitly "white" attributes I might add) are the only ones included. Cardullo writes that "Mr. Webb seems to be in favor of equal treatment for everyone, but in reality he is playing to his audience's prejudice that blacks and newly arrived European immigrants belong at the bottom of the socioeconomic ladder" (78).

Now Cardullo's argument suggests that Wilder's play embraces the ideas espoused by Editor Webb, but I would argue that *Our Town* critiques such attitudes. Does Wilder tell "bourgeois audiences exactly what they want to hear, but in a way that makes them think they are discovering something new or startling" (Cardullo 85), or does Wilder create a highly idealized, nostalgically seductive village—a bastion of whiteness—only to point out how cold, unfeeling, and unappealing such a place is? The answer, I think, is found in *Our Town*'s lack of scenery.

According to Dyer, to be white is to be unmarked, unspecified, unseen, and, therefore, universal. As an ideal, however, whiteness "can never be attained, not only because white skin can never hue white, but because ideally white is absence: to be really, absolutely white is to be nothing" (78). Therein lies the paradox of whiteness, and Wilder brilliantly dramatizes this incongruity in *Our Town* by estranging white, middle-class subjectivity. In essence, Wilder critiques whiteness by making it strange and therefore visible. He does this by forcing his audience to come to terms with what is not shown. The first words of Wilder's script are these:

No curtain.
No scenery.
The audience, arriving, sees an empty stage in half-light. (5)

Unlike the bourgeois materialism so prominently displayed in the 1930s Broadway productions of Eugene O'Neill's *Ah, Wilderness!* and Howard Lindsay and Russell Crouse's *Life with Father,* audiences entering the Henry Miller Theatre were immediately unsettled by what was not on view. The absence of normal theatrical signs disrupted their need for a fixed sense of place and time.

Wilder's insistence that his play not contain scenery or props was a challenge for many in his audience. In one negative review the *New York Journal American* critic John Anderson found the play cold and dispassionate, "an illustrated lecture without the illustrations" (16). Writing for the *New Yorker,* Robert Benchley was affected by the work, but he also declared that "playing it half in speech and half in dumb show, half with real chairs and half with imaginary lawnmowers and string beans, adds nothing to its value" (26). *Catholic World* critic Euphemia Van Rensselaer Wyatt was most succinct: "Personally we resented the shabby ugliness of the chairs and tables" (729).

This negative reaction to the perceived "shabbiness" of Wilder's and director Jed Harris's experimental staging moves us closer to a more complete understanding of the playwright's use of irony. *Our Town*'s lack of scenery was a not-so-subtle challenge to a 1930s Broadway audience that desired its theatre to be nothing more than, in Wilder's words, "an inconsequential diversion" (Wilder viii). Indeed, *Our Town* strikes at the heart of American bourgeois complacency. For Wilder the middle class "were benevolent within certain limits, but chose to ignore wide tracts of injustice and stupidity in the world about them; and they shrank from contemplating those elements within themselves that were ridiculous, shallow, and harmful. They distrusted the passions and tried to deny them. Their questions about the nature of life seemed to be sufficiently answered by the demonstration of financial status and by conformity to some clearly established rules of decorum" (Wilder ix). If one reads *Our Town* through these words, it becomes a subversive play whose ironic stance is intimately tied to the dominant discourse it contests. Specifically, that discourse is the white, Anglo-Saxon, Protestant ideal.

This idea is particularly borne out in the third act, when Emily pleads for one last return to her beloved Grover's Corners. Wilder calls for ten or twelve ordinary chairs to sit on the stage-right side of the proscenium. This is the cemetery where Emily will soon find herself. In Harris's original production the stage was filled with actors dressed in black. The dead were sitting in the chairs, and the undertaker and mourners stood stage-left huddled together and holding black umbrellas. Wilder's stage directions read:

Suddenly EMILY *appears from among the umbrellas. She is wearing a white dress. Her hair is down her back and tied by a white ribbon like a little girl. She comes slowly, gazing wonderingly at the dead, a little dazed. She stops halfway and smiles faintly. After looking at the mourners for a moment, she walks slowly to the vacant chair beside Mrs. Gibbs and sits down.* (55)

Here, in death, Emily is transcendent in a white dress and ribbon amid the sea of black costumes and surrounded by the unadorned walls of the theatre space. But Emily is no Little Eva, a nineteenth-century theatrical representation of feminine purity unsullied by the dark drives that reproduction necessitates. Emily does not enshrine the desirability of whiteness but provides an unsettling, disruptive image of white motherhood. Emily has died during the birth of her second child. She is not innocent, yet she is not knowing either. Her desire to return to the past and revisit a happy childhood memory allows Wilder the opportunity to dramatize the pitfalls of nostalgic desire, for Emily's visit makes her sadder than does death itself.

Emily chooses her twelfth birthday, and Wilder and Harris provided 1930s audiences with a theatrically strange scene that articulated the most extreme representation of whiteness in *Our Town*. Again, Wilder's stage directions read:

The stage at no time in this act has been very dark; but now the left half of the stage gradually becomes very bright—the brightness of a crisp winter morning. (58–59)

Indeed, Emily has chosen a cold, snowy morning to return to. She delights in seeing an "old white fence that used to be around our house" (59) and overhears Constable Warren talking to the milkman about a group of Polish immigrants who got "drunk and lay out in the snowdrifts" (59). Entering her house, however, Emily is frightened by hurried parents—their "*movements and voices are increasingly lively in the sharp air*" (60)—who cannot move slowly enough for her to take them in. "I can't. I can't go on," she pleads. "We don't have time to look at one another" (62).

This scene disturbs the very idea of the tranquil, egalitarian community that so many have read into Wilder's play. In a moment in which lighting design, costumes, and text come together to cast a harsh light over the stage, the inhabitants of *Our Town* are revealed as pressured, emotionally reserved, and controlling. "That's what it was to be alive," says the caustic Simon Stimson: "To move about in a cloud of ignorance; to go up and down trampling on the feelings of those . . . of those about you. To spend and waste time as though you had a million years. To be always at the mercy of one self-centered passion, or another.

Now you know—that's the happy existence you wanted to go back to. Ignorance and blindness" (63).

In the final moments of his play Wilder appears to be begging his audience not to look back in times of trouble and not to turn to representations of America that deny racial and ethnic minorities. In a time of anxiety and crisis Wilder asks his primary audience—the middle- and upper-class majority—to move beyond the shallow banalities of material comfort and financial status and to find significance in the present human condition. I believe Wilder held a mirror up to nature that, ironically, reflected a generation squandering its immense potential. Wilder's *Our Town* offers a troubled, uniquely modern vision of a world torn between the vestiges of the past and an unknown, somewhat frightening, but potentially compassionate future.

Works Cited

Anderson, John. "*Our Town* Lacks Play, Scenery." Review of *Our Town*, by Thornton Wilder. *New York Journal American*, 5 February 1938, p. 16.

Atkinson, J. Brooks. Review of *Our Town*, by Thornton Wilder. *New York Times*, 5 February 1938, p. 18.

Benchley, Robert. Review of *Our Town*, by Thornton Wilder. *New Yorker*, 12 February 1938, pp. 26, 28.

Bhabha, Homi K. "Slant: The White Stuff." *Artforum* 36.9 (1998): 21–24.

Bigsby, C. W. E. *A Critical Introduction to Twentieth-Century American Drama, 1900–1940*. Vol. 1. Cambridge: Cambridge University Press, 1981.

Bordman, Gerald. *The Oxford Companion to American Theatre*. 2d ed. New York: Oxford University Press, 1992.

Cardullo, Bert. "Whose Town Is It, Anyway? A Reconsideration of Thornton Wilder's *Our Town*." *College Language Association Journal* 42.1 (1998): 71–86.

Coleman, Robert. "*Our Town* Presents Life Cycle in a Village." Review of *Our Town*, by Thornton Wilder. *New York Sunday Mirror*, 6 February 1938, p. 34.

Dyer, Richard. *White*. London: Routledge, 1997.

Fergusson, Francis. "Three Allegorists: Brecht, Wilder, and Eliot." *Sewanee Review* 64 (1956): 544–73.

Franchey, John. "Mr. Wilder Has an Idea." *New York Times*, 13 August 1939, sec. 9, p. 2.

Gottfried, Martin. *Jed Harris: The Curse of Genius*. Boston: Little, Brown, 1984.

Hutcheon, Linda. *Irony's Edge: The Theory and Politics of Irony*. London: Routledge, 1994.

Lockridge, Richard. "The New Play: Thornton Wilder's *Our Town* Opens at Henry Miller's Theatre." Review of *Our Town*, by Thornton Wilder. *New York Sun*, 5 February 1938, p. 28.

Miller, Jordan Y., and Winifred L. Frazer. *American Drama between the Wars: A Critical History*. Boston: Twayne, 1991.

Porter, Thomas E. *Myth and Modern American Drama*. Detroit: Wayne State University Press, 1969.

Savran, David. *Breaking the Rules: The Wooster Group, 1975–1985*. Ann Arbor: UMI Research Press, 1986.

Sievers, W. David. *Freud on Broadway: A History of Psychoanalysis and the American Stage*. New York: Hermitage, 1955.

Watts, Richard, Jr. "The Theaters: New England Town." Review of *Our Town*, by Thornton Wilder. *New York Herald Tribune*, 5 February 1938, p. 6.

Wilder, Thornton. *Three Plays by Thornton Wilder: "Our Town," "The Skin of Our Teeth," "The Matchmaker."* New York: Bantam, 1957.

Wyatt, Euphemia van Rensselaer. "The Drama." Review of *Our Town*, by Thornton Wilder. *Catholic World* 146 (March 1938): 724–32.

There Shall Be No Night and

the Politics of Isolationism

Barry B. Witham

I N THE CONTROVERSY surrounding the 1989 Southwest Missouri State University production of Larry Kramer's *The Normal Heart*, playwright and Missouri native Lanford Wilson wrote an editorial for the *Springfield (Mo.) News-Leader* about the nature of live theatre that is among the most articulate and inspiring documents of the late twentieth century. In the face of AIDS hysteria and rampant homophobia Wilson warned his readers:

> Let it be known to all those who have for some reason not known it previously, that theatre is rated "X." You are not safe here. The theatre is for those people who are willing to be challenged, who expect to be challenged. . . . Don't go to the theatre to be titillated, go to be shocked, good and healthily. Go to be moved intelligently and honestly and with integrity. . . . Expect us to be straight with you, it's the last place where we can be. Don't come to the theatre expecting us to conform to the community standards of morality. That's not our job. We would rather die first. If you can't stand up under the mandate of art, turn on the television set. Go to a movie. Stay home. (Wilson)

Lanford Wilson's notion of "X" rated is fundamental to a great deal of political theatre in the previous century: theatre that is not content to reflect events but rather engages and challenges them, theatre that participates in the life processes of a society and collaborates in the manufacture of ideology that characterizes and sustains that life, theatre that does matter.

One of the most vivid examples of such political theatre is Robert Sherwood's now nearly forgotten *There Shall Be No Night* (1940). Winner of the Pulitzer Prize in drama, *Night* was directly inspired by the impending war in Europe, specifically the Russian invasion of Finland, and its performances were terminated when Hitler's attack on the Soviet Union threatened to turn the "reds" into American allies. Between these two events, *There Shall Be No Night* participated in the campaign to turn the United States away from isolationism and pull it into a great second war on the European continent. Seldom has one Broadway production both reflected and manufactured attitudes about war and peace.

The turnabout on Sherwood's part from arch isolationist to advocacy for violent action was stunning in itself but was also typical of the journey that many Americans had taken in the late thirties. As author of several antiwar plays Sherwood had repeatedly made the case against war, terming it God's version of solitaire (*Idiot's Delight*) and exposing how appeals to nationalism and the profits of arms manufacturers frequently lead men and women into descents of savagery. Few scenes were as vivid to many theatregoers—and as preposterous to some—as the climactic moment of *Idiot's Delight* when the Lunts stood atop the European world and sang "Onward Christian Soldiers" while the bombs announcing the outbreak of the Second World War rained down from above.

But that was 1936, and a majority of Americans believed deeply that the country had no business fighting in another European war. The League of Nations had been rejected. Many were convinced that Hitler could be appeased, and if he wasn't, well, perhaps he and Stalin could devour each other. It is difficult to recapture the fervor of those years, but Sherwood himself, gassed at Ardennes, wanted to make sure that America remembered the lessons of the First World War. The incredibly brutal trenches, the deadly explosions from tunneling under the front lines, the agony of the dying, the gas, the mud, the rats. Even Roosevelt, the class enemy to many because of his far left leanings, was forced to promise that no American boys would be sent to die in European wars.

And Congress was filled with statesmen, charlatans, and orators who would hold the president to his promise. Wheeler, Borah, Johnson, Pittman all supported neutrality legislation and pushed for more. William Manchester relates how Representative Louis Ludlow of Indiana introduced a resolution that stated the authority of Congress to declare war would be legal only if it received a majority affirmation in a nation-wide referendum. Polls suggested that the public supported the resolution, which garnered 209 votes in the House and failed only because it fell short of the required two-thirds majority (Manchester 177). Fortress America was powerful and persuasive. Gallup polls as late as 1939 reported that 90 percent of Americans would fight if the country were invaded but only 10 percent would bear arms on foreign soil (Manchester 201).

By 1939, however, many liberals were having second thoughts. As Hitler continued to rail against the Jews and communists within and against his neighbors without, and as the cries for "living space" became more strident, the threat of a totalitarian Europe seemed a real possibility. Sherwood had moved away from his avid isolationism in *Abe Lincoln in Illinois,* confronting those historical moments when waging war is the only alternative, but he still clung desperately to his hatred of violence. On the eve of Chamberlain's humiliation at Munich, Sherwood wrote in his diary, "This is one of the most exciting days in the history of the world. Another message last night from President Roosevelt, this one solely to Hitler and putting the finger precisely on him . . . conference tomorrow in Munich. . . . Who can say now that Woodrow Wilson lived and died in vain, that all died in vain who fought to make the world safe for democracy" (qtd. in Brown, *Worlds* 384).

His hopes were dashed, of course, as the betrayal and invasion of Czechoslovakia ignited the war and the subsequent Hitler-Stalin pact unmasked the ambitions of the Soviet Empire. But it was not Hitler who forced Sherwood into *There Shall Be No Night.* It was the Russian invasion of Finland and the "Winter War" of 1939–40 that finally moved one of America's most respected dramatists to articulate the failures of pacifism and the need for armed resistance.

Finland, like the United States, was a neutral country, but unfortunately it shared a border with Russia and provided access to Leningrad. In addition it had only won independence from Russia two decades earlier, and Stalin was anxious to reclaim and use Finland to secure his western defenses. It was relatively easy to cobble up a "revolutionary government" and stage a fake border incident, and the Red Army could be loosed on the Finns. On 30 November 1939 Helsinki was bombed, and the Russians struck along the Karelian Peninsula and into the "waist" of the country. It was supposed to be a decisive and quick victory.

But from the outset the war was a series of disasters for the invaders. The weather was brutally cold and remained so for nearly three months. Russian tanks and armored vehicles skidded along the narrow roads and were attractive targets for guerrilla attacks. Supply lines were continually broken by the hit-and-run Finn ski commandos, and the Russian wounded agonized in the cold that froze their morphine. The Finns who had anticipated the attack lay in wait and then counterattacked on three fronts, stalling the invasion and sending masses of Russians in full-scale retreats into the forests. Fighting continued for days and then weeks. American correspondents and radio reporters arrived to report the war back to the United States. The Finns awaited and then pleaded for help from the Western democracies to aid them in this unprovoked battle.

Sherwood listened to the reports and agonized about this latest brutality. "I was terrified of identifying myself as a 'Warmonger.' But my mind was settled principally by two events: the first was a speech in October by Colonel Charles A. Lindbergh, which proved Hitlerism was already powerfully and persuasively represented in our own midst; the second was the Soviet invasion of Finland" (Sherwood xxvii). For Sherwood the image of the brave Finns holding out against the hordes of the Red Army while the rest of the world just watched was powerful tonic. On Christmas night, 1939, he heard a particularly moving radio piece from Helsinki by W. L. White on CBS and determined to act. He decided to write a new play about the invasion of Finland, a play so contemporary that its outcome might be changed at any moment. And he intended to rush it into rehearsal so that its scenes would be taking shape at the same time as the events on the Finnish border. It was a bold venture not just because he was drawing from life but because he intended to mount his own campaign, to preach to his fellow Americans that their once-revered isolationism was suicidal.

Sherwood began writing as the Finns surrounded and then carved up the Russian 163rd and 44th Motorized Divisions, inflicting some five thousand casualties and seizing dozens of tanks, trucks, and artillery.[1] Sherwood did not know very much about Finland, but he knew that Alfred Lunt did, and it was Lunt, along with Lynn Fontanne, whom he wanted for the production. They were currently on tour with *Taming of the Shrew,* which was to close in New York in February, and Sherwood set 10 February 1940 as the deadline for what he hoped would be his second full draft. Through a series of encircling movements, the Finns cut off a large part of the Soviet Ninth Army on January 6, and two weeks later they were able to sever all supply lines to the 168th Division, bringing the invasion to a virtual standstill. Sherwood had by this time mapped out the action and created most of the characters. Lunt would play Dr. Valkonen, a Nobel Prize–winning scientist and pacifist who would be thrust into the position of having his principles tested when

---

[1] There are a number of helpful accounts of the "Winter War." I have drawn here on H. M. Tillotson (1993), who is among the most authoritative.

the Russians invade his country. Eventually his own son would be swept up in the conflict, and Valkonen would be forced to choose between fighting or annihilation.

Sherwood finished the first draft in late January amid news reports that the Finns were desperate for support from their Western allies. They had stopped the invasion, but their ranks were dangerously thin, and the Russians had huge reserves to throw into the battle. France sent arms, but the United States and Britain demurred. Sherwood was furious and returned to the task. On February 2 he wrote in his diary, "The Finns are still holding the Russians magnificently, but I'm slow" (Brown, *Ordeal* 61). And the next day, "I hope it is good. It could be an 'influence'" (61).

On February 6 the Russians counterattacked, sending the Seventh and Thirteenth Armies into the Karelian isthmus, threatening the Finnish defenses along the Mannerheim line. A week later the Russian 35th Tank Brigade nearly broke out, and the Finns prepared for an assault on the city of Viipuri. Sherwood, working furiously on his second draft, set his fifth scene in a Helsinki hotel, where war correspondent Dave Corween and his friends listen to reports of the Russian forces attacking across Viipuri Bay. Seldom had a political play resonated with such contemporary events, and seldom had an American play been so closely intertwined with the events it was dramatizing.

Sherwood finished the second draft with Viipuri still under attack. The play now had seven scenes, four of which were set in Dr. Valkonen's home in Helsinki, and covered a period from October 1938 to the present. The action was clear and direct, and each episode served to dramatize Dr. Valkonen's movement from pacifist to engaged combatant. Beginning with his radio speech denouncing Hitler in the first scene and his opposition to his son's fighting against the Russians, Valkonen is subjected to the hostility of the invaders, the passion of his daughter-in-law's defense of country, the courage of American volunteer ambulance corps, and the death of his son. Ultimately he delivers a powerful speech about opposing the Russian invaders and picks up a gun to participate in the final battle. At home in Helsinki his wife also refuses safe passage to America with her new grandchild and vows to defend her home with force if necessary. But the story is not what is most intriguing about *There Shall Be No Night*. What is fascinating is the way that Sherwood uses the characters and episodes to mount his own attack on American isolationism, to focus the play on converting his audiences away from their misguided attitudes about "fortress America."

Sherwood conducts his campaign on three fronts. First, the play repeatedly draws parallels between Finland and America. Valkonen's wife

Miranda (played by Lynn Fontanne) is from New Bedford, Massachu-
setts, and their home in Helsinki looks very much like an American
home that audiences would recognize immediately. Moreover, its walls
are decorated with portraits of Miranda's ancestors that collectively illustrate the growth and power of the United States. In his opening
radio address Dr. Valkonen sends his personal regards to the Mayos in
Minnesota because their state "is so much like Finland, with many beautiful lakes, and forests of birch and pine and spruce. And I know so
many fine people there, with good blood that come from Finland"
(Sherwood 22). Dave Corween, the American correspondent who has
seen the capitulation at Munich and who will cover the fall of Warsaw,
gives frequent voice to Sherwood's linkage of America and Finland.
"Finland is a country with a population about equal to that of Brooklyn," he announces in his first broadcast, and "it has made democracy
work. It has no minority problems. . . . Its people are rugged, honest,
self-respecting and civilized" (17). Comparing Finland with Munich,
Corween exclaims, "You don't know what it means to be in a really free
country again. To read newspapers that print *news*—to sit around cafes
and hear people openly criticizing their government. Why—when I saw
a girl in the street who wasn't afraid to use lipstick, I wanted to go
right up and kiss her" (10). Erik, the Valkonens' son (played by Montgomery Clift), argues that it is his American blood that gives him the
courage to resist and that it was Americans who taught the whole world
what was worth fighting for. Pointing to one of the portraits on the
wall, Erik tells his mother, "I have the same blood in me that you have—
the blood of that gentleman up there. . . . He fought with Jackson at
New Orleans" (53).

Having established the link between the two "democracies," Sherwood raises the stakes for his audiences by showing that the threat is
not just to the Finns. He wants Americans to understand that what is
being played out across Viipuri Bay is part of a much larger threat. For
those liberals who championed the Soviet Union (as Sherwood himself
once did), the attack reveals their hypocrisy. "Three months ago," says
Corween, "the Soviet troops marched in. . . . They thought it would be
a grand parade through Finland, like May Day in Red Square. So now—
several hundred thousand men have been killed—millions of lives have
been ruined. The cause of revolution all over the world has been set
back incalculably. The Soviet Union has been reduced from the status
of a great power to that of a great fraud" (170). And Corween rails
against the propaganda of the Red Army as they broadcast greetings
to the "workers" in Finland. "Never, again," exclaims Corween, "will
these workers of the world arise" (131).

But in Sherwood's campaign it is not sufficient to just discredit the Russians. The real lesson of this Winter War is that it exposes the Russians as cat's-paws for the Nazis, the real enemies of freedom everywhere. Time and again Sherwood drives his point home. A fighter pilot spots German officers advising the Russian attacks; an ex-patriot ridicules those who believe that Hitler can be mollified. And in perhaps the most blatant moment, the German consul general in Finland explains patiently to Dr. Valkonen that the greatest race the world has ever known is being formed and that they will use whatever means necessary to conquer the world. "The Finnish incident is one little item in our vast scheme. We make good use of our esteemed allies in the Soviet Union. . . . [T]hey are working for us, although they may not know it. Communism is a good laxative to loosen the constricted bowels of democracy. When it has served that purpose, it will disappear down the sewer with the excrement that must be purged" (86).

And in the face of this terror, what is the American response? Sherwood's third front is to shame his audiences by confronting them with their lethargy and their ignorance. Ziemsman, the German consul observes that "the United States is secure for the present. It may continue so for a long time, if the Americans refrain from interfering with us in Mexico and South America and Canada. . . . They are now showing far greater intelligence in that respect than ever before. They are learning to mind their own shrinking business" (89). Strong words for those who espoused the notion of Fortress America. When he is asked what is going on at home while the Finns are dying, Corween replies that Southern Cal has won the basketball championship and that the Beaux Arts Ball was an outstanding success (136). And in one of the most controversial moments in the play Corween tells a Polish pilot who has idolized the United States,

> It isn't always so completely delightful to be an American, Major. Sometimes even we have an uncomfortable feeling of insecurity. I imagine that Pontius Pilate didn't feel entirely at peace with himself. He knew that this was a good, just man, who didn't deserve death. He was against a crown of thorns on principle. But when they cried "Crucify Him!" all Pilate could say was. "Bring me a basin of water, so that I can wash my hands of the whole matter." (122)

Pacifism was no longer acceptable for the impassioned author of *There Shall Be No Night,* and in his fervency for his task he equated it with the ultimate betrayal.

The play went into rehearsal in late February. Lunt had agreed to direct, as well as to play Dr. Valkonen. He assembled a remarkable cast, including Sydney Greenstreet, Thomas Gomez, and Richard Whorf, along with Fontanne and the young Montgomery Clift. The rehearsals were electric as Lunt infused the company with his own personal passion about Finland. Although the Lunts had a long history of not being necessarily "political," they were both deeply committed to the struggle for Finland and had been active in the Finnish Relief Fund, which had been organized in January and was supported by donations from a number of Broadway shows.[2]

The production was scheduled to open in Providence on 29 March 1940 and then on to Boston, Baltimore, and Washington before an April 29 New York premiere. On March 13, however, the Finns officially capitulated and a cease-fire was declared. Although Viipuri had not fallen and Helsinki had not been occupied, the Finns were exhausted, outnumbered, and outgunned. The Russians redrew their border with Finland and proclaimed a victory. But the journey for the company of *There Shall Be No Night* was just beginning.

The first week in February 1940 had been declared Finland Week, and Broadway producers and actors had been encouraged to donate salaries and funds to support the Finnish struggle. On the surface it seemed a good enough idea, but isolationist politics quickly turned it into a battleground. Those supporting the Finns were declared "warmongers," threatening to drag the United States into armed conflict in Europe. Those opposed to the fund were branded "communists" because of their refusal to take sides against the Soviet Union. By the time Sherwood's play opened in Rhode Island, the argument was heated. Lillian Hellman and her star in *The Little Foxes,* Tallulah Bankhead, were openly feuding. The theatrical unions were complaining about actor "donations," and name-calling had replaced civil discourse.

The production was cheered in the out-of-town tryouts in spite of an occasional newspaper attack on their "warmongering," and the New York opening was a sensation. Reviewers observed that the play was talky and flawed, but the Lunts were widely acclaimed as magnificent and the company as superb. The *Daily Worker* hated the play—along with the *Daily Mirror*—and it was picketed by a variety of groups and individuals including the ultra-left Theatre Arts Committee, but the passion of the work overwhelmed audiences. Moreover, Hitler's winter attacks into Denmark and Norway revitalized the timeliness of Sherwood's message and made an even more compelling case for the play's interventionist stance.

---

[2]For a recent discussion of the politics involving the Fund see Amy Taiple (1999).

There Shall Be No Night ran for six months to sold-out houses, and then Sherwood took his campaign on the road. In November the company began to tour, playing across the United States and into Canada. Everywhere they encountered opposition, but audiences flocked to see the production. The premier of Canada, MacKenzie King, told the Lunts that the play encouraged him to speak candidly with Americans about the approaching war. Eleanor Roosevelt was so moved by the performance that she applauded the cast and author in her newspaper column. In May Sherwood was informed that he had won the Pulitzer Prize.

The company took a break for the summer, intending to continue the tour and then reopen in New York in February 1942. But events were moving very swiftly now and overtaking *There Shall Be No Night*. London was under attack, and Roosevelt was providing aid under the guise of "lend-lease." In June Hitler double-crossed the Russians and invaded the Soviet Union. The American Communist Party that had been urging neutrality had to shift its policies once again now that it was allied with the United States against the Nazis. In October the company resumed its tour and discovered that its "warmongering" was now being praised by the *Daily Worker*. The Playwright's Company, which was producing the play, grew nervous about its anti-Soviet politics. In addition, the Finns—lacking support from the Western democracies—had signed a pact with Germany. On 7 December 1941 the Japanese attack on Pearl Harbor rendered the whole debate academic.

The Playwrights Company—of which Sherwood was a prominent member—announced that "the best interests of this country would be served through the termination of the tour" (Jared Brown 296). Two weeks after Pearl Harbor the play closed in Rochester, Minnesota. Sherwood had succeeded beyond his fantasies in helping to turn the country away from its isolationist policies, but his work had been overtaken by the realignment of national interests and the rush to war. In spite of a Pulitzer Prize, *There Shall Be No Night* was now impolitic to present.[3] Today it is a museum piece, its power diminished. Accessing it is like traveling to a foreign country. But for a moment in the 1940s it was X-rated, cheered, and vilified. It was, in the words of Alfred Lunt, "something like playing in Uncle Tom's Cabin before the Civil War" (Jared Brown 293).

---

[3] In 1943 Sherwood produced an updated version of the play in London that focused on Fascist attacks in Greece. For a comparison of the two texts see Joki and Sell (1989).

Works Cited

Brown, Jared. *The Fabulous Lunts.* New York: Atheneum, 1986.

Brown, John Mason. *The Worlds of Robert Sherwood: Mirror to His Times.* New York: Harper and Row, 1962.

———. *The Ordeal of a Playwright.* New York: Harper and Row, 1970.

Joki, Ikka, and Roger Sell. "Robert E. Sherwood and the Finnish Winter War: Drama, Propaganda and Context 50 Years Ago." *American Studies in Scandanavia* 21 (1989): 51–69.

Manchester, William. *The Glory and the Dream.* New York: Bantam, 1974.

Sherwood, Robert. *There Shall Be No Night.* New York: Charles Scribners, 1940.

Taiple, Amy L. "Broadway and the Finnish Relief Fund: Politics at the End of an Era." *Theatre Studies* 44 (1999): 5–18.

Tillotson, H. M. *Finland at Peace and War.* Norwich, Great Britain: Michael Russell, 1993.

Wilson, Lanford. "If You Can't Stand Honest Theatre, Stay Home." *Springfield News-Leader,* Insight Section, 12 November 1989, B1.

Contributors

Carol Burbank is Assistant Professor of Theatre and Performance Studies at the University of Maryland, College Park. She researches the connections between political theatre and activist movements and is currently revising a book manuscript, *Ladies Against Women: Feminist Activism, Satirical Theatre and the Politics of Gender in the Late 20th Century*. Dr. Burbank performs her own Ladies Against Women character in the tradition of the originators of the technique and teaches workshops in parody and comic performance. Her other interests include developing interactive Web-based learning programs, contemporary adaptations of classic theatre works, and adapting nonfiction for the stage.

Jonathan Chambers is Assistant Professor of Speech and Theatre at St. Lawrence University in New York; he teaches performance studies and acting. His areas of interest include early-twentieth-century American drama, specifically the theatre of the political left; the acting technique and theory of Michael Chekhov; the historical avant-garde, specifically methods of performance; current nonrealistic drama; and melodrama as a period acting style. His articles have been published in *Victorian Studies* and *Theatre History Studies*.

Steve Earnest teaches in the Theatre Department at California State University, San Bernardino. He is a member of both Actor's Equity and the Screen Actor's Guild. His professional acting credits include the Burt Reynolds Theatre in Jupiter, Florida; the Colorado Shakespeare Festival; the Beverly Hills Playhouse; and several film and television projects, including *Miami Vice*. His articles have been published in the *O'Neill Review, Western European Stages, Theatre Journal, Journal of Dramatic Theory and Criticism,* and *Contemporary Theatre Studies*. His book on the State Acting Academy of East Berlin was published in December 1999 by Mellen Press.

Kurt Eisen is Associate Professor of English at Tennessee Technological University, where he specializes in modern American drama. His book on Eugene O'Neill, *The Inner Strength of Opposites,* was published by the University of Georgia Press in 1994.

James Fisher, Professor of Theatre at Wabash College, has authored four books, held several research fellowships, and published articles and reviews in numerous periodicals. He edits *The Puppetry Yearbook* and is book review editor for the *Journal of Dramatic Theory and Criticism*. Dr. Fisher is the 1999–2000 McLain-McTurnan-Arnold Research Scholar at Wabash and was named "Indiana Theatre Person of the Year" by the Indiana Theatre Association in 1996. He is currently completing books on the early productions of Edward Gordon Craig and the plays of Tony Kushner.

Anne Fletcher is Associate Professor of Theatre at Winthrop University in South Carolina. She received her Ph.D. in Theatre History from Tufts University. Her dissertation was on Group Theatre designer Mordecai Gorelik. A chapter from her master's thesis was published in the *Secondary School Theatre Journal* and her reviews have appeared in the *New England Theatre Journal* and *Theatre Journal*. Dr. Fletcher currently serves on the board of the South Carolina Theatre Association and is secretary to ATHE's Theatre History focus group.

Christopher Herr is Assistant Professor of English at California State University, Los Angeles, where he teaches courses in both the English Department and the Department of Theatre Arts. In addition to research work in theatre history and dramatic literature, he has worked as a playwright, director, and actor and is one of the founding members of North Coast Theatre, an experimental company based at the Toledo (Ohio) Museum of Art. His book, *Clifford Odets and American Political Theatre,* is forthcoming from Greenwood Press's *Lives of the Theatre* series.

Susan Kattwinkel is Assistant Professor of Theatre at the College of Charleston in South Carolina, where she teaches theatre history and literature, dramaturgy, and stage management. She received her Ph.D. from the University of Texas at Austin. Her anthology of vaudeville afterpieces, *Tony Pastor Presents: Afterpieces from the Vaudeville Stage* was published in 1998, and she is currently editing a volume of essays on audience participation (forthcoming from Greenwood Press in 2001). Dr. Kattwinkel has received two development grants from the College of Charleston, one to develop a Web site for her theatre history and literature classes and one to conduct research during the summer of 2000 in New York on changing social mores as reflected in the vaudeville theatre.

John O'Connor is Assistant Professor of Theatre at Fairmont State College in West Virginia. He contributed a chapter on Howard Brenton to *British Playwrights, 1956–1995: A Research and Production Sourcebook,* edited by William Demastes, published in 1996 by Garland Press. In 1998 he presented at the International Society for the Study of European Ideas Conference.

Mary Trotter is Assistant Professor of English at Indiana University–Purdue University at Indianapolis. She received her Ph.D. in theatre and drama from Northwestern University. She has published on such topics as Irish women playwrights, the Field Day Theatre Company, and *The Playboy of the Western World* riots in the journals *Theatre Survey* and *New Hibernia Review* and in the books *Crucibles of Crisis: Performing Social Change* (1996), *The Cambridge Companion to British Women Playwrights* (forthcoming), and *Widening the Stage: A Century of Irish Theatre* (forthcoming). Her book, *Inventing Irish Theatre,* a historical and critical study of the diversity of nationalist theatre and performance practices during the Irish literary renaissance is forthcoming from Syracuse University Press in spring 2001.

Jeff Turner teaches theatre studies at Maryville College in Maryville, Tennessee. He has studied acting with Anne Bogart and worked professionally as an actor, director, and dramaturg with the Colorado Shakespeare Festival and the North Carolina Shakespeare Festival.

Barry B. Witham is Professor of Theatre at the University of Washington in Seattle. In addition to his academic work he was dramaturg for the Seattle Repertory Theatre from 1983–87, where he helped develop a number of new plays. He has been a consultant to the Biography series on A&E television and is coauthor of *Uncle Sam Presents* (University of Pennsylvania Press, 1982) and editor of *Documents of Theatre in the United States* (Cambridge University Press, 1996). Dr. Witham has received outstanding teaching awards from two universities and is a member of the National Theatre Conference and the College of Fellows of the American Theatre.

Editors

John C. Countryman is the Director of Theatre and Associate Professor at Berry College in Georgia. His new play, *The Leather Man or the End of the Road,* was produced in November of 1999 by the Berry College Theatre Company. He serves as an associate editor for *The Journal of Dramatic Theory and Criticism.* His articles appear in numerous journals, including *Theatre Symposium,* the *ACA Bulletin, Threshold,* and *Irish Studies Working Papers.* Dr. Countryman has received numerous grants, including a Fulbright Scholar-in-Residence Award to bring Albanian playwright Arben Kumbaro to Berry College during the 1999–2000 academic year. He studied ancient theatres in Italy and Greece during the summer of 2000. He is the 1997 recipient of Berry's Carden Award for outstanding teaching, scholarship, and service.

Noreen Barnes-McLain is Associate Professor and Director of Graduate Studies of Theatre at Virginia Commonwealth University in Richmond, Virginia. Her previous experience includes serving as dramaturg and assistant for Joseph Chaikin on several productions and workshops and directing the premiere of Kate Bornstein's *Hidden: A Gender,* Brad Fraser's *Unidentified Human Remains and the True Nature of Love,* and Alan Ball's *Five Women Wearing the Same Dress.* Her research interests include women in nineteenth-century Anglo-American theatre and gender and sexuality in performance.